"Thank you again for defusing what might have turned into an even more unpleasant situation, Mr. Sinclair."

"You're always so polite while you're trying to get rid of me." He smiled, a slow curving of the lips that gave his strong-featured face a devastating appeal. "What's it going to take for you to call me Rory?"

Peggy slicked her tongue along her bottom lip. She didn't want to picture herself in his arms, breathing his name against his heated flesh, but she did. "I think..." Her voice hitched, and she cleared her throat. "It would be wise for us to keep things between us on a business level, Mr. Sinclair."

He said nothing for a moment, but stared down at her with those off-the-chart blue eyes until she had to fight the urge to squirm.

"You're right," he said softly. "That would probably be the *wise* thing to do...."

D0726031

About the Author

MAGGIE PRICE

Viewing the world from behind the badge of an FBI special agent hero wasn't a giant step for Maggie Price to take. A former civilian crime analyst for the Oklahoma City Police Department, Maggie possesses an insider's knowledge of cops and the workings of various law enforcement agencies. Add to that her having snagged assignments to several task forces alongside FBI special agents, and it was only natural that FBI forensic scientist Rory Sinclair would stride onto the pages of *Protecting Peggy* as a true-to-life cop with a microscopic eye for detail and a cop's dangerous edge.

Maggie loves to hear from readers! Contact her at 5208 W. Reno, Suite 350, Oklahoma City, OK 73127-6317.

Protecting Peggy

Maggie Price

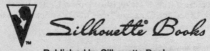

Published by Silhouette Books

America's Publisher of Contemporary Romance

If you purchased this book without a cover you should be aware
that this book is stolen property. It was reported as "unsold and
destroyed" to the publisher, and neither the author nor the
publisher has received any payment for this "stripped book."

Special thanks and acknowledgment are given
to Maggie Price for her contribution
to THE COLTONS series.

SILHOUETTE BOOKS
300 East 42nd St.,
New York, N. Y. 10017

ISBN 0-373-38716-4

PROTECTING PEGGY

Copyright © 2001 by Harlequin Books S.A.

All rights reserved. Except for use in any review, the reproduction
or utilization of this work in whole or in part in any form by any
electronic, mechanical or other means, now known or hereafter
invented, including xerography, photocopying and recording, or in
any information storage or retrieval system, is forbidden without
the written permission of the editorial office, Silhouette Books,
300 East 42nd Street, New York, NY 10017 U.S.A.

All characters in this book have no existence outside the imagination of
the author and have no relation whatsoever to anyone bearing the same
name or names. They are not even distantly inspired by any individual
known or unknown to the author, and all incidents are pure invention.

This edition published by arrangement with Harlequin Books S.A.

® and TM are trademarks of Harlequin Books S.A., used under license.
Trademarks indicated with ® are registered in the United States Patent
and Trademark Office, the Canadian Trade Marks Office and in other
countries.

Visit Silhouette at www.eHarlequin.com

Printed in U.S.A.

THE COLTONS

*Meet the Coltons—
a California dynasty with a legacy of privilege and power.*

Rory Sinclair: *Not the marrying kind.* Having dedicated his life to researching chemical and biological warfare for the FBI, he's not about to be distracted from his current mission. Until he comes head-to-head with a toothless toddler and her beautiful mother...

Peggy Honeywell: *Feisty single mom.* When a town emergency forces a federal agent to move into her bed-and-breakfast, this proud widow suddenly has trouble remembering all the reasons she'd vowed to avoid dangerous men at all costs.

Samantha Honeywell: *Heartbreaker-in-waiting.* This wise two-year-old knows that any man who'd rescue a tattered pink bunny is a keeper!

Michael Longstreet: *Beleaguered mayor.* As the town of Prosperino faces its water crisis, he's about to be tested in life—and love.

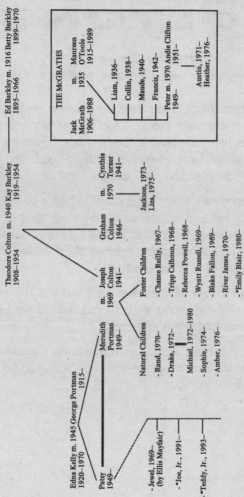

THE COLTONS

Theodore Colton m. 1940 Kay Barkley
1908–1954   1919–1954

Ed Barkley m. 1916 Betty Barkley
1895–1966   1899–1970

THE McGRATHS

Jack McGrath   m. Maureen O'Toole
1906–1988   1935   1915–1989

- Liam, 1936–
- Collin, 1938–
- Maude, 1940–
- Francis, 1942–
- Peter m. 1970 Andie Clifton
  1949–   1951–
  - Austin, 1971–
  - Heather, 1976–

Graham Colton 1946–

m. Joseph Colton 1969 1941–

m. Cynthia Turner 1970 1941–
- Jackson, 1973–
- Liza, 1975–

Foster Children
- Chance Reilly, 1967–
- Tripp Calhoun, 1968–
- Rebecca Powell, 1968–
- Wyatt Russell, 1969–
- Blake Fallon, 1969–
- River James, 1970–
- *Emily Blair, 1980–

Natural Children
- Rand, 1970–
- Drake, 1972–
- Michael, 1972–1980
- Sophie, 1974–
- Amber, 1976–

Meredith Portman 1949–

Edna Kelly m. 1945 George Portman
1920–1970   1915–

Patsy 1949–

- Jewel, 1969– (by Ellis Mayfair)
- *Joe, Jr., 1991–
- *Teddy, Jr., 1993–

LEGEND
- - - Child of Affair
▮ Twins
● Adopted by Joe Colton

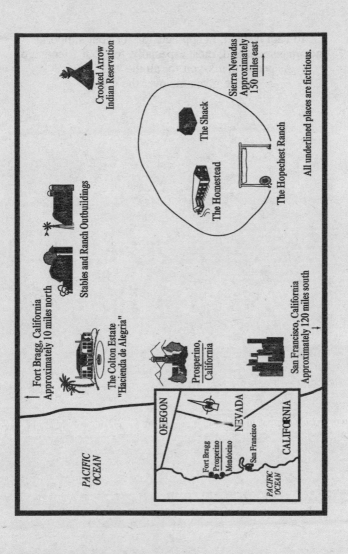

PACIFIC OCEAN

Fort Bragg, California
Approximately 10 miles north

Stables and Ranch Outbuildings

The Colton Estate
"Hacienda de Alegria"

Prosperino,
California

San Francisco, California
Approximately 120 miles south

Crooked Arrow
Indian Reservation

The Shack

The Homestead

The Hopechest Ranch

Sierra Nevadas
Approximately
150 miles east

All underlined places are fictitious.

OREGON

NEVADA

CALIFORNIA

Fort Bragg
Prosperino
Mendocino
San Francisco

PACIFIC OCEAN

To Pam Newell, in appreciation for your support,
encouragement and, most especially, for your friendship.
A special thank-you for all the "kid" advice
you've given me over the years.

One

As a member of the FBI's elite evidence support team, Rory Sinclair's hopping a flight from D.C. without much advance notice usually meant he was headed to a crime scene. His rainy-night arrival in California wasn't the case, although he'd stowed his computer and field evidence kit in the trunk of the car he had rented three hours ago at the San Francisco airport. For the first time in years, Special Agent Rory Sinclair was off the Bureau's clock and on his own time.

Time, that Rory had agreed to spend posing as a civilian chemist while conducting a surveillance at a widow's homey bed-and-breakfast.

With rain slanting down through the darkness, the sign welcoming Rory to Prosperino—a town hailing itself as a tourist's mecca on the rugged northern California coast—glistened in the car's headlights.

From what Rory could see of the flower-laden planters and neat benches that lined the sidewalks in front of a row of darkened storefronts, Prosperino looked picture-postcard perfect, everything calm and serene. Untroubled.

The urgent call Rory had received the previous day from Blake Fallon, his former college roommate, told Rory there was at least one imperfection on Prosperino's charming facade. That imperfection came in the form of the mysterious contamination of the water supply on Hopechest Ranch, the haven for troubled adolescents and teens where Blake served as director. The contamination had occurred weeks ago. Since then, Blake had watched a series of Hopechest's staff and residents fall ill while the EPA inspector assigned to the case conducted his investigation at a suspicious snail's pace.

Peering through the rain-spattered windshield, Rory spotted the road to Honeywell House marked on the map Blake had faxed him. Braking, he turned, then steered along a thin ribbon of road that curved up a hill. Although Rory had Blake's assurances that the widow Honeywell ran a first-class establishment, comfort wasn't the reason Rory was headed there. EPA Inspector Charlie O'Connell had checked into Honeywell House weeks ago. Rory wanted a close look at the man who had raised Blake's suspicions by conducting at least one clandestine meeting on Hopechest Ranch property.

Honeywell House was impressive, Rory decided as he drove past a wooden sign that welcomed him to the inn. Small spotlights spread dramatic fans of illumination across the face of the building that nestled against the hillside. Inside, lights burned gold behind windows dotting four stories, the upper one ringed by a widow's walk.

Rory pulled the car into the gravel lot at the side of the house and climbed out, thankful that the rain had slowed to a light mist. When he turned to walk toward the back of the car, he noted the outline of a small greenhouse sitting a few yards away.

He retrieved his leather duffel bag, computer and field kit out of the trunk, then headed up the water-beaded cobblestone walk. He took the steps two at a time that led up to the large, wraparound porch. Although he'd never given much thought to his surroundings, something compelled him to turn and look back toward the road he'd just driven. The inn sat high enough on the hill that, past the wash of light from the streetlamps, he could see a wedge of the rocky cliffs that edged the fierce, churning Pacific. Mrs. Honeywell, he mused, had herself a piece of prime real estate.

Pushing open the inn's carved double doors, Rory left the chilling mist behind him. A mix of scents wafted in the warm air—lemon, cinnamon and lavender. The foyer was spacious with waist-high oak wainscoting from which colorful wallpaper rose. A handsome mahogany reception counter sat in the center of a gold and cream tapestry rug that pooled over the polished wood floor.

Through an archway to his left he glimpsed a study lined with shelves crowded with books. The room had a high ceiling, wood floor and a green-marbled fire-place in which flames fed on thick logs that burned

with a woodsy smell. The plump leather couch in front
of the hearth looked like a great spot to curl up with a
book.

He doubted he would have time to do that on this
trip.

Turning his attention back to the foyer, he noted the
brass plaque inscribed "Private" affixed to the wall
beside a door that stood partially ajar.

Rory settled his bags against the wall, took two steps
toward the reception desk, then halted when a deep
voice coming from behind the door said, "There's no
need to put your back up just because a man pays you
attention."

"That kind of attention isn't welcome," a woman
responded. "Touch me again, and you and all of your
belongings will be out in the street. You have my word
on that."

Rory arched a brow. The woman's voice was as
steady as the January mist that shrouded the inn. With
an ample spicing of temper.

Shifting his stance, he peered through the doorway
into what appeared to be a small office. He could see
one side of a bookcase, a file cabinet and a portion of
a desk. It was the woman standing at the front of that
desk, facing sideways, who commanded his attention.
She was medium height with a delicate build, squared
shoulders and creamy skin that held the trace of a flush.
An angry flush, Rory theorized, considering the tone
of her voice. Her dark hair fell, wave after wave, over
the shoulders of her vivid turquoise sweater; the hem
of a long black skirt skimmed her calves.

When the owner of the bass voice stepped closer to

the woman, he moved into Rory's line of sight. The man was tall and solid with a square jaw and sharp eyes. Judging from the brown hair just going to gray, Rory put his age at forty-something. He wore brown slacks and a tan sweater, its sleeves shoved up on his well-developed forearms.

"I didn't come in here meaning to upset you." Although the deep voice had softened, Rory caught the hard edge to the words. "Look at it this way, we're both unattached. We have mutual needs. What's the harm in helping each other satisfy those needs?"

"The only need you can help me satisfy is to leave this office. That way I can start getting my inn settled for the night."

My inn. Rory pursed his mouth. Because Blake had referred to the bed-and-breakfast proprietress as "the widow Honeywell who cooks like an angel," Rory had been expecting an apron-clad, homey woman with gray hair tucked into a bun. Peggy Honeywell was anything but homey and looked to be in her late twenties. He wondered vaguely what had happened to the husband who had died and left her such a young widow.

As if sensing his presence, she turned her head toward the door. Rory saw surprise flicker in her expression when her gaze met his. Even from a distance he could see that her wide-set eyes were the color of rich emeralds.

She looked back at the man. "This discussion is over. Excuse me while I see to a customer."

The man flicked an idle glance across his shoulder at Rory, then looked back. "I'll be staying here at least another week. Let me know when you change your mind.''

"I won't. Good night, Mr. O'Connell.''

Training kept Rory's expression unreadable as he slid the keys to his rental car into one pocket of his leather bomber jacket. Small world, he thought. That the guy putting moves on the Widow Honeywell was Charlie O'Connell, the EPA inspector whom Rory had come there to surveil.

Peggy Honeywell swung the door open and moved into the foyer with a dancer's grace. "I didn't hear you come in.'' Her gaze slid to the bags Rory had settled against the wall. "I'm sorry, I don't have any vacancies.''

"Blake Fallon made a reservation for me. I'm Rory Sinclair.''

"Oh, yes, Blake said you'd be in tonight.'' Her mouth curved. "Since you planned to drive up from San Francisco, I was expecting you later.''

"I managed to catch an earlier flight out.''

"That's fortunate.'' Rory sensed her hesitate before offering a hand. "I'm Peggy Honeywell, Mr. Sinclair. Welcome to Honeywell House.''

When his fingers curved around hers, Rory felt flesh as smooth as soft butter...and the heat of the angry flush that still rode high on her cheeks.

Out of the corner of his eye, he saw that O'Connell had stepped from the office and was now leaning in the doorway. The man's brow furrowed as he gazed down at the hard-sided field evidence kit Rory had settled against the wall beside his duffel bag and computer.

Rory turned, extended his hand. "Rory Sinclair."

O'Connell looked up, then pushed away from the doorjamb. "Charlie O'Connell." The inspector's handshake was dry and firm. Decisive. "What brings you to Prosperino, Sinclair?"

"I'm a chemist. Blake Fallon hired me to conduct independent tests on the water at Hopechest Ranch. Blake shut down the well there nearly two weeks ago. He's anxious to find out what contaminated the water. And how it got there."

Rory saw the instant caution kick into O'Connell's eyes. "Getting answers to questions like those takes time."

"True." To cement his cover, Rory added, "According to Blake, with so many people having gotten sick, it's possible the ranch might face some lawsuits down the line. The attorney for the Hopechest Foundation, which owns the ranch, wants independent testing done on the water." Rory angled his head. "How about you, O'Connell? You vacationing in Prosperino?"

"Hardly. I'm an inspector with the EPA. The contamination on Hopechest Ranch is my case. My jurisdiction."

Rory kept his expression somber. "I'm not looking to step on anyone's toes."

"See that you don't."

Setting his jaw, Rory watched O'Connell turn and cross the foyer.

"I'm sorry," Peggy said after the inspector shut the inn's front door behind him with a snap.

Rory turned his head, gazed down into her eyes. He

imagined any number of men would be happy to permanently lose themselves in all that intriguing jade. Not him. He was a man for taking, enjoying and moving on. "What are you sorry for?"

"Mr. O'Connell has been a guest here for two weeks. At times, he can be decidedly unpleasant."

Like when he's trying to put the make on you. "I don't see that you need to apologize for him."

"You're right, of course." When she looked toward the small, private office, her mouth tightened, reminding Rory of the temper he had heard in her voice. "He's responsible for his own actions. I just regret he directed his bad mood toward another of my guests."

Rory shrugged. "Slid right off."

"Good." She shoved her dark hair behind her shoulders. "I'm sure you're tired from your flight and drive. It will just take a minute to get you registered," she added, then turned and walked to the registration counter, the long sweep of her skirt matching her flowing stride.

"Fine."

"Blake told me the purpose of your visit, Mr. Sinclair."

"Rory."

She gave him a slight smile as she stepped behind the counter and slid open a drawer. "The whole town is holding its breath until we find out what contaminated the ranch's water. Several pregnant teenage girls who live at the ranch drank tainted water. Now, they fear for the health of their unborn babies."

"Blake mentioned those girls." For Rory, hearing that was all it took to request the use of some of the massive amount of personal leave he'd accrued, pack his field kit, then head west.

"Mayor Longstreet assures us Prosperino's water supply is tested daily, still we're all nervous," Peggy said. "The grocery stores can't keep enough bottled water on hand to supply everyone, including me."

"That's understandable." Rory stepped to the counter. "I have my field testing equipment with me. If you'd like, I'll check the inn's water every day while I'm here."

She looked up from the drawer. "I appreciate that. Each morning when I go to the kitchen and turn on the water, I can't help but wonder if what's coming out is okay to drink. To cook with. Bathe in. Knowing for sure would ease my mind. Of course, I'll pay you for the testing."

"That's not necessary. Since I'm a guest here, I have a vested interest in knowing the water is safe."

"All right." She pulled a key and a blank registration card from the drawer, then slid it closed. "All I need is your name and address."

Rory reached for the pen in a brass holder on the counter. He signed his name and address on the card, then looked up. He noted Peggy's gaze had settled on his hands. "Do you want to see my credit card now?" he asked quietly.

When her eyes jerked up to meet his, he saw edgy caution flicker across her face. She was an innkeeper, used to strangers in her home. Yet, instinct told him his presence made her uneasy.

"No, I don't need your credit card. Blake told me to bill the Hopechest Foundation for your room." Pulling her bottom lip between her teeth, she dropped her gaze to the registration card. "I keep a list of where my guests live. You're the first I've had who calls D.C. home."

Throughout his entire thirty-five years, he had called nowhere home, yet Rory didn't see the need to point that out. He was more interested in analyzing what it was about him that made her edgy.

"What about you?" he asked. "Are you a native of Prosperino?"

"Actually, I was born in Ireland."

He angled his chin. She had the dark hair, green eyes and pure creamy skin of her birthplace. "You don't sound like Ireland."

"I didn't live there long." Leaving the card on the counter, she retrieved the key. "I'll show you to your room now."

"Fine." He felt her gaze on him, measuring and assessing, while he retrieved his gear.

"Your room is on the third floor. Do you need help carrying your things upstairs?"

"I pack light." Rory knew the statement summed up his life. The bureau's go-where-you're-sent discipline fitted his lifestyle to a T. He'd never kept—or wanted—anything he couldn't fit in a bag and take along with him.

"I serve breakfast between seven and ten." She moved from behind the counter and started, brisk and businesslike, toward the staircase. "As an amenity to my guests, I provide wine and cheese in the library during the early evenings. If you're interested, I can recommend several restaurants in Prosperino that serve an excellent lunch and dinner.''

"I'll get those from you tomorrow. How many guest rooms do you have?''

"Five." She paused, one foot on the bottom step, her hand on the carved newel post. "January is usually my slow month, except for the winter arts festival. That takes place this week. Two of the judges of the art competition are staying here. There's also a couple spending a few days of their honeymoon with us. You and Mr. O'Connell have the other two rooms."

As she moved up the gleaming oak staircase in front of him, Rory watched the subtle, elegant sway of her hips beneath her black skirt. Peggy Honeywell had one hell of a walk, he decided.

Tightening his grip on his field kit, he told himself to keep his mind on business. "Speaking of O'Connell, I hope I can persuade him to compare notes on what he's found so far on the contaminated water. Are our rooms on the same floor?"

"No, in fact, that's his there," she said as they stepped onto the second-floor landing.

Rory's gaze followed hers to a closed door with a brass 2 affixed to its center. Rory knew Blake well enough to give credence to his suspicions about O'Connell. Still, mere suspicions didn't prove the EPA inspector was up to something nefarious. Also, O'Connell's failure to identify the contaminant in Hopechest's water could be due to its degree of rarity. Rarer substances took longer to isolate. Processes of elimination used in the lab could take weeks to make an ID.

Rory followed Peggy up another flight of stairs. Setting a quick pace, she led him down a hallway painted a soft yellow, its wood floor dark with age and polish. As they walked, they passed an antique credenza holding a pewter bowl from which a spiky-leaved plant sprouted.

When they reached the door at the end of the hall, she slid a key into the lock, then swung open the door. "I hope the room is to your liking."

"It'll be fine." He gave the quilt-covered brass bed, prints of wildflowers on the walls and braided rug on the wood floor a cursory look. His surroundings usually suited him, from the lab in D.C. to his rented Virginia apartment to crime scenes all over the world. This room was no different from the hundreds of others he'd stayed in, then left behind.

It was his landlady who drew his attention as she moved toward a closed door, fingering the room key she'd yet to give him.

"The bathroom is through here," she said, opening the door. "I usually change the linen and towels in the morning. That might not be a good time if you're planning on working here."

"Mornings are fine."

Nodding, she slicked her palms down her thighs. "The closet is over there."

Eyeing her steadily, Rory settled his gear on the bed. He couldn't shake the feeling that his presence made her jumpy. "Do I make you feel uneasy, Mrs. Honeywell?"

"Of course not," she countered, then paused while a faint flush crept up her throat. "I'm sorry if I gave you that impression, Mr. Sinclair. I'm a little distracted, is all."

"Mind if I ask by what?"

"I promised myself I would work on my income taxes this evening. Just the thought of tackling all those forms makes me jittery."

He gave her a smooth smile. He didn't believe her for one minute. "That's understandable."

"Well, if you'll excuse me, I have to set up for breakfast before I tackle the paperwork." She glanced around the room, then walked toward him. "Your key also fits the lock on the front door. You'll need it to get into the inn after nine at night. I hope you enjoy your stay. Let me know if there's anything you need."

"I will." Deliberately, he let his fingertips glide against hers when he accepted the key. As a scientist, it was his nature to try to logic out the intangible. As a man, he was becoming increasingly intrigued by her reaction to him.

"Good night, Mr. Sinclair."

"Please call me Rory. Good night."

When she turned away, a faint trace of her subtle flowery scent slid into his lungs.

He watched her go, continued staring at the door after it clicked shut behind her. He'd been wrong, he thought. This room *was* different from the hundreds he'd stayed in over the years. For the first time in his memory, a room he'd checked into smelled as softly sweet and alluring as a woman.

The thought triggered a quick, inner defense signal in Rory's brain. He hadn't checked into Honeywell House to sniff at the landlady, he reminded himself as he went through the automatic routine of unpacking his leather duffel. Granted, he would have to be in a coma not to appreciate Peggy Honeywell's slim figure, emerald-colored eyes and lustrous dark hair that framed her gorgeous face. And, as a man who spent his life solving puzzles, her reaction to him made him curious. Damn curious.

All normal responses to a beautiful, intriguing woman, he assured himself. Still, just because the demands of his job had prevented him from being with a woman at all for some time, that didn't mean he was going to allow himself to start thinking about the landlady with the mind-set of a randy teenager. He intended to keep his thoughts on the sole reason he had checked into Honeywell House.

Charlie O'Connell.

Rory furrowed his brow as he began setting up his computer and preliminary testing instruments on the small writing desk that sat opposite the bed. It had been evident the EPA inspector wasn't happy that Hopechest had hired a private chemist to test the ranch's water. Could be, O'Connell simply resented the fact that the EPA's failure to ID the contaminant had prodded Blake Fallon to take action. Then again, if O'Connell had something to hide, Rory knew his presence would have sounded an alarm in the inspector's head to which O'Connell would react.

That, Rory thought, was a reaction he planned to watch for closely. And, while he was watching O'Connell, he would keep his eyes and his thoughts off Peggy Honeywell.

* * *

Good Lord, Peggy thought as she leaned against the wall just outside the door to Rory Sinclair's room. Weren't scientists supposed to be harmless-looking people who wore thick glasses, used pocket protectors in their white coats and had pale skin from being shut up in sterile labs?

That description didn't come close to the man she'd just snapped the door shut on! Rory Sinclair was tall and lanky, with jet-black hair, a tanned, narrow face hardened by prominent cheekbones and killer blue eyes. His looks—combined with the fact that he'd been dressed all in black—had made her think of a highwayman who'd checked into her inn to take a break for the night from pillaging the countryside.

And the women who lived there.

Peggy closed her eyes. She pictured his hands, those long elegant fingers as he'd signed his name and address across the registration card. Somehow, someway, she had known, just by looking at his hands, how they might feel if he touched her.

"Get a grip, Honeywell," she muttered.

Shaking her head, she pushed away from the wall and set off down the hallway. What was wrong with her? Just because a man's hard features and dark clothes made him look absurdly dangerous didn't mean he was. Rory Sinclair was Blake Fallon's friend, a scientist who had come to Prosperino on legitimate business—which in no way encompassed him putting his hands on her.

She blew out a breath, having no idea where that crazy thought had come from. No doubt, the man had a wife and a couple of kids back in D.C., she reminded herself. Since it was getting late, she needed to rein in her imaginings and direct her attention to her own business, which included setting up for breakfast.

Her newest guest had caught her off-guard was all, Peggy reasoned as she reached the top of the staircase. When she'd first glimpsed Sinclair standing in the foyer, she had thought for the space of a heartbeat that he might be a ghost. After all, she hadn't heard him open the inn's front door. Hadn't been aware of his footsteps as he crossed the foyer's wooden floor. Yet, there he'd stood, watching in silence while she dealt with lecherous Charlie O'Connell. However mild Sinclair's expression, she had seen in his eyes a quick and thorough measuring of the situation he'd walked in on.

How many times had she looked up and found Jay standing only inches away from her when she hadn't even heard him walk into the room? How often had she seen her husband conduct the same instinctive evaluation of his surroundings as had Rory Sinclair?

Although she had used her skittishness over tackling her taxes as an excuse for her unease around Sinclair, she admitted to herself that her instinctive comparison of him to her late husband had knocked her off-balance.

Starting down the stairs, she pushed away the dull pang of the memory. Jay had been dead nearly five years; even after so long she sometimes wondered if the scars of grief she carried in her heart would ever completely heal.

She had healed, Peggy reminded herself as she shoved her hair behind her shoulders. She had carved out a new life for herself and Samantha. Her business was thriving—if she kept an eagle eye on the budget she would have two guest rooms added on to the inn before the end of the year. In her mind, expansion marked success.

Her mouth quirked when she reached the bottom of the staircase. She supposed she should give thanks that Rory Sinclair had arrived when he did. Successful inn-keepers offered their guests openhanded hospitality, not slaps to the face like the one she'd been tempted to deliver to the EPA inspector.

Remembering the way Charlie O'Connell had slunk into her office, trapping her between the desk and his body while his hands gripped her waist had her temper spiking all over again. It took a real Neanderthal to assume that just because a woman was a widow she was lonely for a man's touch. Granted, it had been a long time since she had stepped into a man's arms, but that was by choice. If she decided she wanted physical contact, she was relatively sure she could make that happen.

Brow furrowed, she moved across the foyer into the book-lined study. Her gaze swept the oak floor, dotted by hooked rugs, then the small tables scattered about, checking to make sure everything was in place.

Satisfied with the state of the room and that Samantha hadn't left any of her toys lying around, Peggy moved to the green-marble fireplace. There she crouched, her gaze going to the flames that ate greedily at the dry wood. Only to herself would she concede that on nights like this, when the wind turned sharp and a cold mist shrouded the inn, she felt her aloneness intensely. It was only human to long for someone to hold her, to again have a man to share her life with.

She knew she could pick up the phone, call Kade Lummus—a sergeant on the Prosperino Police Department—and he would come running. Kade was a good-looking man whose open expression and friendly brown eyes invited trust. More than once he had made it clear he was interested in getting to know her on a personal level. If she allowed herself to, she suspected she could become interested in him. Yet, that wasn't going to happen. She had buried one husband who died because he wore a badge. That was enough for a lifetime.

She was twenty-eight; she didn't intend to be alone forever. Someday, Peggy thought, shutting off the gas that fed the flames. Someday she would meet another man to whom she could give her heart. A man who would love her and Samantha equally. A man who didn't have to strap on a bulletproof vest just to try to survive each workday. A man whose family didn't have to wonder when he left each morning if he would walk back through the door that night. A safe man.

As if beckoned by some unseen force, her thoughts went to Rory Sinclair. He was a ruggedly handsome man who had an aura of danger about him, just as Jay had. An aura that had drawn her inexorably to the only man to whom she had given herself and her heart.

Never again, she vowed. The next time she got involved with a man, she wanted safe.

She was determined to have it, both for the sake of herself and her daughter.

Two

A persistent, unending droning penetrated Rory's thoughts, dragging him from a deep sleep. When he pried his eyes open and waited for his brain to clear, he realized the noise was the wind. A brisk wind that battered the lace-covered windows that let in a gray morning gloom.

For the first time in longer than he could remember, he lingered in bed. He wasn't sure what kept him beneath the colorful quilt and crisp sheets that he suspected had been ironed. Maybe it was an uncharacteristic urge to familiarize himself with this one room when he'd never felt the need to conduct more than a cursory study of the hundreds of other unfamiliar places he'd woken in during his career.

He propped his back against the headboard while his gaze slicked over the wallpaper spattered with small

roses, the braided rug that pooled color across the wood
floor, the little porcelain dish that held mints on the
bedside table. His brow furrowed. No, he decided, it
wasn't the room itself. Although he appreciated ambi-
ance, he never took much notice of it, especially in a
place where he didn't plan to spend any measurable
length of time. What had snagged his attention was the
woman who had created the setting that he now examined as if it were evidence under a microscope. The
woman whose flower-delicate scent clung to the linens
that enveloped him in warmth.

For a brief instant, Rory wondered what it would be
like to have that woman lying naked beneath him, her
dark hair spread across his pillow, those compelling
green eyes smoky with desire.

"Dangerous thought, Sinclair," he muttered. Although he had spent little time in Peggy Honeywell's
presence, instinct told him she wasn't his type. He pre-
ferred quick, uncomplicated contacts. Women who
laughed and loved without any thought for the future.
Because with him, there was no future.

Shoving back the covers, he settled his feet on the
cool wood floor and moved his gaze slowly around the
cozy room. The woman who had created this setting
had clearly put down roots and sunk them in deep. He
doubted there would be anything quick or uncomplicated about an affair with her.

Peggy Honeywell was on his mind solely because
he was curious to find out what it was about him that
made her so damn jumpy. After all, he was a man who
loved solving puzzles.

So, what was the key to *this* puzzle? he mused while

he headed to the bathroom. Why had she acted so uneasy in his presence?

His profession? he speculated, then instantly discarded the notion. She had no idea he was FBI. No clue he carried a gun and a badge. He doubted her knowing he was a scientist carried even an inkling of a threat.

A threat. Rory ran a palm across his stubbled jaw as he stared into the mirror over the sink. Maybe it hadn't been *him* at all. Could be, she was even more concerned over the state of the inn's water supply than he had picked up on. She was, after all, a single woman who, he assumed, supported herself. Her livelihood could come to a screeching halt if she had to close Honeywell House if its water supply became contaminated.

Turning on his heel, Rory went to the small desk opposite the bed. There, he retrieved a test tube and indicator strips from his field evidence kit. Last night, before he went to bed, he had checked the inn's water and found no trace of a contaminant. It was time to run another test.

That way he could give the dark-haired, green-eyed Peggy Honeywell some peace of mind.

"I'm gonna draw a picture of Bugs."

The mention of the beloved stuffed rabbit had Peggy sending her four-year-old daughter a smile from across the kitchen's center island. As was their habit in the mornings while Peggy cooked breakfast for the inn's guests, Samantha had climbed up on one of the long-legged stools, her crayons and drawing paper fanned out in front of her.

"Drawing a picture of Bugs is a great idea, sweetheart. The other day I found an empty frame in the storage closet. We'll put your picture of Bugs in it and hang it in your bedroom."

"Okay." Samantha's smile lit up her small face, with its pointed chin and pert nose, its big brown eyes mirroring the color of rich earth. Her thick jet-black curls hung past her shoulders, giving her the look of a gypsy.

Samantha selected a crayon that matched the bright pink quilted jumper she wore. "Do you think the lady in the booth can paint Bugs on my cheek tomorrow night? Maybe Gracie's, too?"

"Probably," Peggy said soberly. "But it might not be as good a picture as yours."

"I know," Samantha said with confidence. Her face set in concentration, she got down to work.

While Peggy used a long-handled wooden spoon to stir the second batch of pancake batter of the morning, she stifled a yawn. Because she'd spent most of the night tossing and turning, just the thought of the long day that lay ahead had fatigue pressing down on her. Thank goodness the winter arts festival wasn't until tomorrow night, she thought. She had promised to take Samantha and her best friend, Gracie Warren, for a return visit to the face-painting booth they had discovered at last year's festival. Peggy knew the girls would want to stay until the festival closed.

With the batter smooth of lumps, she turned to the window where colorful pots of herbs lined the sill. After examining the spearmint, she snipped off several sprigs to use for garnish on the serving platters. Instead of turning back to the bowl of batter, she let her gaze focus out the window.

The day had dawned gray and gloomy with a fierce wind that tormented the trees lining the ribbon of road that led up the hill to the inn. Lying awake in bed, she had known the exact moment the wind had intensified, sweeping in with its battering gusts and mournful howl. For some reason she couldn't explain, the instant she heard that howl, loneliness had begun scraping at her like tiny claws.

She had not felt such a deep, hollow ache since those terrible days after Jay died nearly five years ago.

Pulling her bottom lip between her teeth, Peggy rinsed the sprigs of spearmint, then laid them on a paper towel to dry. Maybe the reason she felt so uncharacteristically empty was that Rory Sinclair had reminded her so much of the husband she had loved and lost. For that reason, too, it was only natural she hadn't been able to put the tall, lanky scientist out of her mind.

Until right now, she resolved as she turned to the center island and poured the pecans she'd chopped earlier into the bowl of batter. She had guests to feed, rooms to clean and orders to place with two food distributors and a local winery. After four years, the running of the inn and the chores that went with it were so ingrained that they normally left her brain free to think about anything that struck her fancy.

Although musing about a man with the tough, intense face of a warrior might be pleasurable, she wasn't going to allow herself that diversion. Her relationship with Jay had taught her that she was a woman readily drawn to a man with an aura of danger about him. She had no intention of again letting herself be tantalized by a man like that. Especially one who was just passing through.

"Good morning."

Peggy's stomach gave an intriguing little flip at the sound of Rory Sinclair's voice. She looked up to find him with one shoulder propped against the doorjamb, his dark gaze focused on her in total concentration. He looked impossibly handsome in black jeans and a gray polo shirt, its sleeves shoved up on his forearms. His jet-black hair glistened wetly from what she assumed was his morning shower.

"Good morning, Mr. Sinclair."

"Rory."

She gave him a cool smile even as heat crept up her neck. How long, she wondered, had he been standing there watching her and Samantha?

"There's coffee in the dining room. Two of the guests—the ladies who are judging categories in the winter arts festival—are already there." Peggy inclined her head toward the doorway opposite from the one in which he lingered. "You can get to the dining room through that door. I'll serve breakfast in about fifteen minutes."

"Whatever you're cooking smells great." Rory strolled across the kitchen, pausing when he reached the side of the center island from where Samantha sat eyeing him, the pink crayon gripped in a fist that had gone motionless above the paper.

"Momma's making pancakes with nuts in 'em. They're my favorite."

"Pecans," Peggy amended. "And cinnamon-apple sausage to go with the pancakes." Since she was adamant about her daughter learning manners, Peggy added, "Samantha, this is Mr. Sinclair. He checked in last night after you were in bed."

Having grown up in an inn constantly filled with strangers, there was nothing shy about the way Samantha scooted the piece of paper his way. "Do you like my picture, Mr. Sink...Mr. Sinkle?"

He smiled. "I think 'Rory' is a much easier name. It's a great picture, Samantha." He tilted his head. "How old are you?"

"Four," she replied, holding up the accompanying number of fingers. "I'll be five in May. What do you think my picture is of?"

Peggy raised a brow as he bent his head to examine the pink, misshapen drawing. Samantha had a habit of using her artwork to test the guests. Ordinarily, Peggy would have chided Samantha into *telling* what it was she was drawing, but for some reason she was curious to see how Rory Sinclair handled the situation.

"It's a bunny," he answered gravely. "With long, pink eyelashes."

Samantha's smile beamed like sunshine. "His name's Bugs. Someday I'm going to have a real bunny. My momma says we'll have to see about that. Now I have to draw Bugs a carrot 'cause he's hungry." Laying the pink crayon aside, she plucked an orange one, furrowed her brow, then started coloring.

Peggy lifted her gaze, met Rory's blue one. "And I

have to finish breakfast 'cause my guests are hungry.
As I said, there's coffee in the dining room."

"And two lady art judges. I got all that the first time
around." He glanced down. "Samantha, are the ladies
in the dining room going to judge your picture, too?"

"No, Momma wants to hang this one in my room."

"Well, it would have been a sure winner. It's a really
good picture."

"I know." She paused, looking suddenly thoughtful
as she stared up into his face. "Do you have a little
girl, too, Mr. Rory? I could draw a picture for her
room."

"No. I don't have a little girl *or* a little boy."

"You're not as lucky as Momma, then."

"Clearly, I'm not," he commented while Samantha
shifted her attention back to the carrot.

Leaning a hip against the island, Rory moved his
gaze to the copper pots and baskets hanging from
hooks overhead. His attention then went to the butcher-
block counters and oversized range and huge refrigerator behind where Peggy stood. "Nice kitchen, Mrs.
Honeywell."

"Thank you." In an unconscious gesture, she ran
her fingertips across the island's dark granite top.
"This was my grandmother's house."

"Was she born in Ireland, too?"

Peggy was vaguely surprised he remembered her
brief mention of her birthplace. Jay had also been
skilled at filing away small details about people.

"No. My birth mother lived in Ireland. I was
adopted by an American couple when I was four

months old.'' Her mouth curved. "Gran used to say I was a special gift from the Emerald Isle.''

"With eyes to match.''

Was it simply her imagination that his voice had lowered, become richer? "I…used to come and stay with Gran in the summers," she continued, trying to ignore the jump in her pulse. "I spent hours in here helping her cook, my mouth watering from all the delicious scents. This room always felt so homey to me. The whole house, in fact. I want my guests to feel that Honeywell House is more a home than an inn.''

His eyes narrowed. "*Do* they feel that way?''

"Most say they do." She tilted her head. "When you check out, maybe you'll let me know your take on the subject.''

"You'll want to ask someone other than me about homey feelings. I tested the inn's water last night and this morning.''

She blinked. His sudden change of subject had her mentally stumbling to catch up. Putting a hand to her throat, Peggy shifted her gaze to her daughter. Samantha hunched over her drawing, the point of her small tongue caught between her teeth while she put the final touches on Bugs's oversize carrot.

A wave of uneasiness swamped Peggy. Despite reassurances from city officials, she had spent countless hours worrying about the town's water supply and wondering if she should take her daughter out of harm's way until the crisis was resolved.

"Is the inn's water safe?''

"Yes. Everything checks out.''

She closed her eyes. Opened them. "Thank you, Mr. Sinclair."

"You're welcome."

"It's been two weeks since they found out the water on Hopechest Ranch was contaminated. Some of the kids who drank it are still sick."

"Do you know any of those kids?"

"No. I've only been to Hopechest a few times because the inn keeps me so busy. I do know, though, that Blake Fallon is terribly worried about those kids." As she spoke, Peggy resumed stirring her pancake batter. "After the agony he went through last year over his father, this is the last thing Blake needs."

"What agony?"

Peggy looked up. "I thought you said you and Blake were friends."

"We are." A look of unease slid into Rory's blue eyes. "We've been friends for a long time."

"Well, it sounds as if you have some catching up to do."

"You're right. I have an appointment to see him after breakfast."

Nodding, Peggy decided to voice the concern she'd had since shortly after the EPA inspector checked into Honeywell House. "Charlie O'Connell claims there's no way to predict how long it might take to find out what it was that contaminated the ranch's water supply. And how it got there."

Rory settled a palm on the counter. "Are you asking me if I agree with him?"

"Yes, I guess I am."

"If O'Connell is conducting his study by the book,

he will have taken water samples at the ranch on the day he arrived in Prosperino. Those samples should have been sent to the EPA lab for analysis. Depending on the rarity of the contaminant, it could take weeks to break down its components and make an ID.''

"That just seems like an awfully long time.''

"I know it does.'' Rory angled his chin. "To put things in context, the breath you just exhaled contains one hundred and two different composites. To conduct a scientific analysis of that one breath, each composite has to be separated, then analyzed. Contaminated water has to be broken down that same way. In a lab, you can't rush tests, can't skip steps. That's why I agree with O'Connell. There's no way to predict how long it might take to find out what it was that wound up in the ranch's water. And how it got there.''

Although she knew next to nothing about Rory Sinclair, instinct told Peggy she could trust what he said. Her gaze went to his hand resting on the countertop, his long, elegant fingers splayed against dark granite. Those long elegant fingers that she somehow knew would work slow, sweet magic against a woman's flesh.

A dry ache settled in her throat. For so many years she had ignored her physical needs. Now those needs seemed to double and triple when she was in the same room with this one man.

"Something wrong?'' he asked quietly.

Peggy looked up, realized he was watching her with the same intense assessment she had seen last night when he walked in on her and O'Connell.

"Of course not,'' she said, pleased that her voice

sounded steady. She ran her palms down the thighs of her gray flannel slacks. "It's just a relief to know the inn's water is safe."

"I'll continue to test it twice a day as long as I'm here."

"I feel guilty not paying you for the testing."

"Well, I don't want your guilt on my conscience." Crossing his arms over his chest, he flashed her a grin. "I'll take my payment in dessert."

"Dessert?" She'd have to be careful of that grin, Peggy told herself. It oozed recklessness and charm. Made you want to put down your guard and relax in his presence. She knew instinctively he was a man it would be unwise to relax around.

"Blake says you cook like an angel and that your apricot cobbler is a direct route to heaven." Rory lifted a shoulder. "I've got a sweet tooth that would like to take that trip."

He didn't look like he had a sweet tooth. He looked incredibly fit, his stomach washboard flat, his forearms toned and muscular. What would it be like, she wondered, to feel that well-maintained body pressed against hers?

The thought brought all of her nerves swimming to the surface. She picked up a jar of herbed vinegar, set it back down. He would not be good for her, she knew that. Still, knowing something wasn't good for you didn't stop you from wanting to sample it.

Which was something she wasn't going to do. A week from now Rory Sinclair might possibly be back in D.C., working in his lab. And, just because he didn't have children didn't mean there wasn't a Mrs. Sinclair waiting for him at home.

That she suddenly found herself hoping he didn't have a wife had Peggy scowling. She had no clue what it was that made her thoughts about one of her guests turn totally idiotic. Whatever it was, she was done with it. She was a professional. A businesswoman.

"It's agreed, Mr. Sinclair," she said in her most efficient tone. "I'll prepare whatever dessert you'd like each evening in exchange for your testing the inn's water every day. Now, if you'll excuse me, I need to deal with breakfast."

He opened his mouth to respond when a loud clatter came from the hallway. An instant later, a masculine voice filled the air with vicious curses.

Panic tripped Peggy's heart. "That sounds like Mr. O'Connell. Samantha, stay here."

Peggy darted to the kitchen door on Rory's heels, raced down the hallway at his side. Just as they reached the foyer, the two caftan-clad art judges burst from the hallway that led to the dining room, the mass of metal and wood bracelets both women wore clanking in unison. When Peggy saw the EPA inspector sitting on the bottom stair, massaging his right ankle, she realized he must have taken a tumble down the staircase.

She rushed to him, placed her hand on his arm. "Are you all right, Mr. O'Connell? Do I need to call a doctor?"

He jerked away, anger shimmering in his eyes as he surged up on one foot and leaned against the newel post. "Dammit to hell, woman, what kind of place are you running here?"

Peggy's chin rose. "One in which you don't have to yell at the top of your lungs for me to hear you. Now, please calm down and tell me how badly you're hurt. Do I need to call a doctor?"

"No, dammit, I don't need a doctor. I need a safety inspector."

Peggy shook her head. "What for?"

"Oh, Bugs!"

Peggy had no idea Samantha had disobeyed her instructions to stay in the kitchen until she heard her daughter's high-pitched wail.

"That's what for." Propping against the banister, O'Connell jerked his head toward the floor at the bottom of the staircase.

Peggy's heart sank when she saw Samantha bent over her beloved pink rabbit, its head torn off and stuffing strewn on the wood floor.

"Damn thing was at the top of the stairs," O'Connell said. "Caused me to slip and fall."

Samantha glared up at O'Connell, tears streaming down her cheeks while she hugged the bunny's torso. "You broke Bugs's head off!"

"Hey, it's a miracle I didn't break my own neck."

Peggy crouched, pulled her sobbing child into her arms. "It'll be okay, sweetheart." She would have to have another stern talk with Samantha about leaving her toys lying around the inn. Now, however, was not the time.

"Your kid's not hurt." O'Connell delivered the words in a steel tone. "I am. You ought to keep that in mind."

Peggy lifted her gaze to his. From where she

crouched, he looked disconcertingly big. And strong. She hated the fact she was nearly kneeling at his feet, but she couldn't do anything about that. Not while Samantha clung to her while she sobbed hot tears against her shoulder.

"It'll be okay, Bugs," Samantha murmured between watery gasps as she rocked the animal. "I'll fix you."

Peggy ran a soothing palm down the child's dark curls. "Mr. O'Connell, I am very concerned about you. Do you need a doctor?"

"A lawyer's more like it."

"I've got a question, O'Connell," Rory said as he stepped between them. Peggy sensed that a protective barrier had suddenly risen in front of her and her child. Still crouched on the floor with Samantha crying against her shoulder, she leaned forward so she could see each man's face in profile.

"What's the question, Sinclair?" the EPA inspector asked.

"Why do you want a lawyer?"

"The kid—"

"Samantha," Rory said evenly. "Her name's Samantha."

"Yeah, well, she left that rabbit in the middle of the stairs. The fall I took could have killed me."

"So, you want a lawyer because you're thinking of suing Mrs. Honeywell?"

O'Connell looked at Peggy. "Maybe." His gaze dropped to her mouth. "Unless we can work out something."

She gritted her teeth while heated anger pooled in her cheeks. If Samantha and her other guests weren't present, she would ask the idiot if he actually thought his threatening her with a lawsuit would compel her to sleep with him.

Rory hooked a thumb in the front pocket of his jeans. "Here's the deal, O'Connell. If you call a lawyer, I'll have to talk to him, too."

A guarded look settled in the man's eyes. "About what?"

"I came down to breakfast ten minutes ago. I saw the pink bunny at the top of the staircase."

"See—"

"Not in the *middle* of the staircase. Off to one side. Against the wall, in fact." Rory shrugged. "Didn't look like a safety problem to me. It sounds more like you just got clumsy. If you had gotten hurt, it would have been your own fault. Besides, what does it say about an *inspector* who trips over something hot pink?"

"We saw the bunny, too, Mr. O'Connell," one of the art judges volunteered while the other nodded in agreement. "This gentleman is right. The bunny was against the wall. You must not have been looking where you were going."

Apparently realizing he was outnumbered, O'Connell scowled. "Yeah, okay. I guess I'm more shaken up than anything."

Peggy swiveled her head, gave the women a grateful smile. "Ladies, would you please escort Mr. O'Connell into the dining room? I'll have breakfast ready in just a few minutes."

O'Connell limped across the foyer between the two women, their bracelets clanking as they each patted one of his arms. Murmuring their sympathies, they steered O'Connell down the hallway that led to the dining room.

Peggy gave Samantha a hug, then settled on the bottom step. "Sweetheart, why don't you take Bugs to your room? While you're at preschool, I'll see if I can sew him back together."

"Can you fix him, Momma?" Voice hitching, Samantha stared at her through swollen, tearful eyes. "Can you really fix him?"

Cupping the small, tearstained face in her hands, Peggy placed a light kiss on her daughter's trembling lips. "I can try."

"Okay." Samantha bent and gathered up the bunny's head. Snuggling it and the fuzzy, pink body against her chest, she headed toward the hallway.

Peggy shook her head. "Dear Lord, give me strength."

Chuckling softly, Rory offered his hand. "All this before breakfast. Are things always this eventful around Honeywell House?"

She hesitated an instant before sliding her hand into his. His flesh felt warm and firm against hers as he helped her to her feet.

"No, thank goodness." Because his fingers had tangled with hers, she took a step back, disengaging her hand from his. "Usually things are on the sedate side." She flicked a look toward the hallway in which O'Connell had disappeared. "I appreciate you stepping in. I doubt I would have been quite so tactful."

"A lioness defending her cub doesn't worry about tact."

Peggy pulled in a deep breath. "No, she doesn't. Samantha comes first with me."

"That's the way things should be."

Peggy knew she had guests waiting for their breakfast, knew she needed to get to the kitchen. Still, she lingered inches from him, the spicy male tang of his cologne pervading her lungs.

"When Samantha showed you the picture she drew, I wondered how on earth you guessed it was a bunny. You knew because you saw Bugs at the top of the stairs."

"The rabbit and the picture are both hot pink." He shrugged. "I made a wild guess."

"An accurate one." She smiled as she fingered a wayward wisp of hair off her cheek. "Thank you again for defusing what might have turned into an even more unpleasant situation, Mr. Sinclair. If you'll join the other guests in the dining room for coffee, I'll see to breakfast."

"You're always so polite while you're trying to get rid of me." He smiled, a slow curving of the lips that gave his strong-featured face a devastating appeal. "What's it going to take for you to call me Rory?"

She slid her tongue along her bottom lip. She didn't want to picture herself in his arms, breathing his name against his heated flesh, but she did. "I think…" Her voice hitched, and she cleared her throat. "It would be wise for us to keep things between us on a business level, Mr. Sinclair."

He said nothing for a moment, just stared down at her with those off-the-chart blue eyes until she had to fight the urge to squirm.

"You're right, Ireland," he said softly. "That would probably be the wise thing to do."

Three

His appetite sated from a breakfast of melt-in-the-mouth pecan pancakes and apple cinnamon sausage, Rory stood in the gravel parking lot that bordered Honeywell House, a hip leaned against the front fender of his rental car. For the past hour he'd been telling himself that he couldn't argue with what Peggy had said before she left him in the foyer. Keeping their dealings on a business level *would* be wise.

He just wasn't sure that wise was the course he wanted to follow.

After all, wise wouldn't get the woman into his arms. Wouldn't have him feeling her ripe, sexy mouth softening and heating under his. Wise wouldn't get her into his bed.

Which would definitely put an enjoyable twist on his stay in Prosperino.

Ireland. Why the hell had he called her that? He'd never before even thought about giving any female a nickname, especially a woman he had known less than twenty-four hours. It was those eyes, he decided. Cool jade that sparked liquid fire when her temper kicked in. Eyes that he suspected would go dark and smoky when she stepped into a man's arms.

His arms.

Frowning, he jerked up the collar of his battered leather jacket. It did little to block the bite of the wind that blustered off the sea churning at the base of the cliff. A thin, damp fog crawled over the gravel parking lot, creeping up the steps that led to the inn's wrap-around porch. The gray morning gloom nearly obscured the small greenhouse that sat only a few yards from the parking lot.

In his mind, Rory pictured again how Peggy had looked when he first walked into the kitchen where the scents of baking had started his mouth watering. Standing there at the work island, dressed in a gray sweater and slacks, her dark hair pulled loosely back with a red ribbon, she had looked outrageously sexy. She'd been stirring pancake batter, for Christ's sake, but that didn't stop a kick of lust from heating his blood.

"Dammit," he muttered.

Crossing his arms over his chest, he gazed at the inn's front porch with a stare as brooding as the gray clouds overhead. When he arrived last night, he hadn't noticed the chairs there, fashioned out of rustic wood or the table covered with a floral, lace-edged cloth. It had been too dark to see the orange and yellow mums that spilled from colorful pots lining the porch's rail.

And the pink bicycle with training wheels that nosed into an alcove away from the front door.

The woman over whom he was currently obsessing had created that welcoming scene. Not only had she made herself and her young daughter a home that apparently kept body and soul anchored, she made a point to create a temporary home for those who passed her way.

A home—even a temporary one—was something he'd never had and he didn't want one now. What he did want—on a short-term basis—was *her*.

"Not going to happen." Even as he spoke the words, the wind snatched them away.

That he was intensely attracted to a woman so unlike those he habitually sought out caused a feeling of unease to creep over him. For months he had been trying to understand the source of a restless discontent that had settled around him. A feeling that his life had somehow gotten a half beat out of synch. This added disquiet over Peggy Honeywell didn't help.

He did, however, understand what it was that drew him to her.

In the world of science, like charges repelled each other. Unlike charges attracted. He was one of the nomads of the world with no roots, no family, no woman waiting for him to return. Just looking at the inn told him Peggy had dug in and was there to stay. She had a daughter to raise, and he would bet that more than a few of Prosperino's male residents had their eye on the innkeeper and their thoughts on a future with her.

Rory knew he couldn't have found a woman more

his opposite if he'd run an ad listing the qualities he preferred to avoid in the opposite sex.

The uneasiness churning inside him hitched up a notch when he thought about the unpleasant consequences of having to disentangle himself from an affair with a woman who put stock in permanence. Common sense told him it would be best for everyone involved if he simply avoided Peggy Honeywell. So, avoid her, he would.

That shouldn't be too difficult since he had plenty on his plate to deal with. Like identifying what substance had contaminated the water on Hopechest Ranch. That unknown substance had sent innocent kids to the hospital and put fear in the hearts of young pregnant girls.

The sobering reality shifted Rory's thoughts to the reason he was now in Prosperino.

Glancing at his watch, he calculated he had a few minutes before he needed to leave for his meeting with Blake Fallon. At breakfast he'd overheard Charlie O'Connell mention to one of the art judges that he had an appointment this morning. Rory figured now was as good a time as any to chat.

Just then, the inn's front door swung open and the EPA inspector stepped onto the porch.

"Bingo," Rory said softly. He narrowed his eyes against the wind and watched O'Connell make his way along the cobblestone walk, his slight limp the apparent aftereffect of his tumble down the stairs. His tan gabardine overcoat hung open over his crimson sweater and khaki slacks. Gusts of wind picked up strands of his brown hair.

Rory waited until his quarry reached the gravel lot before pushing away from the car's fender. "Got a minute, O'Connell?"

The EPA inspector flicked him a look as he walked to a black sedan that displayed the logo of a rental car company on its back bumper. "A minute's about all I have. I'm running late for an appointment."

"I want to talk to you about the water on Hopechest Ranch."

O'Connell twisted the key in the lock, pulled the door open, then turned and met Rory's gaze. "What about it?"

Rory raised a brow. "I don't guess I need to remind you it's contaminated. I'd like to know what your findings are so far."

"I bet you would."

"Meaning?"

Resting a forearm along the top of the car's door, O'Connell pursed his lips. "I don't have time to beat around the bush, Sinclair, so I'll lay this out for you. I've worked a lot of cases where private consultants were involved. It's my opinion you're all alike. You get hired by your client after an investigation is in full swing. You show up in your nice clothes and leather jackets with your state-of-the-art instruments, and expect us government drones to hand over the results of the work we've already done. That isn't going to happen here."

Rory wondered what the man would say if he knew he was talking to a fellow government drone. "I don't expect you to do my work for me, O'Connell. All I'm asking is that you discuss with me what you've found out so far.''

O'Connell flicked an impatient glance at his watch. ''Like what?''

''Hopechest Ranch gets its drinking water from an underground source. Have you made any headway figuring out how the water became contaminated?''

''Not yet.''

Rory took a deep breath. It was clear the man wasn't inclined to share information. Still, he had to try. ''From talking to Blake Fallon on the phone, it sounds like all the victims came down with acute bacterial infections. Has the EPA's lab ruled out the *vibrio cholerae* bacteria? If not, we might be looking at a potential cholera epidemic.''

''We ruled out cholera two days ago.''

''What about traces of mercury in the water? Lead, cadmium, arsenic or beryllium? Find any of that?''

''When I issue my final report, I'll make sure you get a copy.''

''Your final report is considered public record. I can get a copy for myself.''

''I've got to go, Sinclair.''

Rory watched as O'Connell slid into his car, then slammed the door shut. The engine coughed once, then hummed to life.

Despite Blake's suspicions, Rory knew just because the man wasn't forthcoming with information didn't mean he was involved in anything nefarious. In truth, O'Connell sounded like a disgruntled government worker—the FBI's lab had a few of those, too. If, on the other hand, Blake was on target and O'Connell *was*

up to no good, Rory had no clue what the hell that
might be. Or what O'Connell might stand to gain.

Shaking his head, Rory slid into his own rental car.
He knew, like in any other investigation, the answers
would come in their own time.

With Blake Fallon's faxed map on the seat beside
him, Rory steered his car over a narrow bridge that
spanned the rushing Noyo River. He had driven far
enough inland that the fog had dissipated. A heavy
cover of grim, gray clouds still obscured the January
sky, but at least he could now see the countryside.

A neat, white-railed fence lined the curving road that
skirted Hopechest Ranch property; beyond the fence
were rolling hills covered with a thick blanket of grass
where cattle grazed. In the distance, towering redwoods
speared, straight and strong, into the clouds.

Peaceful was the word that slid into Rory's mind as
he glanced at the serene landscape. He frowned, wondering again what it was that compelled him to notice
the scenery when he'd taken so little notice of it for
years.

A sign pointed him toward the turnoff for the ranch's
main entrance; in the distance, several barns, a stable
adjoined by neat, white-railed paddocks and what
looked like a handful of long bunkhouses huddled beneath the gray sky. From his conversation with Blake,
Rory knew that Hopechest Ranch was not only a haven
for kids from troubled homes, but also a full working
ranch with a permanent staff. The thirty to forty kids
who lived there at any given time were all assigned
chores that allowed them to experience the challenges

and triumphs of hard work. In addition to the operation
of a nationally known counseling program, Hopechest
Ranch was home to a school, state-of-the-art gymnasium, archery range and art studio.

Impressive operation, Rory decided as he pulled his
car to a halt beside a sign that identified the adminis-
tration building. Blake had told him the ranch had once
belonged to a private family. The structure in which
Blake both lived and worked had been the family's
dwelling.

That was what it looked like, Rory thought as he
took in the two-story wood-frame house with a porch
that wrapped around two sides and part of a third. The
structure was old, but well-maintained with what
looked to be a fresh coat of white paint and shiny white
blinds in the windows. A thin curl of smoke rose from
the chimney. Just like at Honeywell House, several
chairs and a small table took up one corner of the front
porch.

Rory climbed out of his car and started up the brick
walk. He noted several nearby oaks standing sentinel
just outside the long hedge that bordered the yard. Two
planters on either side of the front door held trimmed
shrubs; beside the door was a discreet brass plaque:
Hopechest.

The reception area was done in gray-blue and ivory.
Polished tables flanked a comfortable-looking couch
upholstered in a dark fabric. The floor was hardwood
and gleaming. A mantelpiece held an antique mirror
and an arrangement of dried flowers. Below it a fire
crackled eagerly.

Behind an uncluttered desk sat a rather plain young

woman who peered at a computer monitor through a pair of understated glasses. She had long, straight brown hair that nearly concealed the phone's receiver she held tucked between one shoulder of her navy blazer and her ear. While she spoke into the phone, her fingers flew across a computer keyboard. The surface of the desk was neatly stacked with printouts and brown accordion files tied with string. The nameplate aligned with the front edge of the desk read *Holly Lamb*. She gave Rory an engaging smile and held up a finger to indicate she'd be with him in a moment.

The smile that lit up her face had him rethinking his initial assessment. She wasn't plain, he realized, not with that classical-shaped face, high cheekbones and perfectly shaped nose. But her skin was bare of makeup, her brownish-green eyes nearly lost behind the lenses of her glasses. He suspected, with the right makeup, the woman would be stunning.

"Mr. Fallon has a meeting that morning," she said into the phone, "but I can give you an appointment for two o'clock the same afternoon." Her fingers paused over the keyboard, then started moving again. "Fine. He'll see you in his office on Wednesday at two."

She smiled up at Rory as she replaced the receiver. "Good morning, may I help you?"

"I'm Rory Sinclair—"

"Oh, yes, Blake's scientist." She rose, tall and slender, moving around the desk with easy grace. The skirt that matched her navy blazer ended just above the knee; her navy shoes were low-heeled and sensible. "I'm Holly Lamb."

"Nice to meet you, Ms. Lamb." Rory returned her firm, brisk shake.

"Holly. We've got our fingers crossed that you'll be able to identify what got into our water."

"I'll do my best."

Her gaze darted to the hallway behind her desk. "I don't think Blake has gotten a good night's sleep since this whole thing started." She looked back at Rory. "It's been awful with so many of the kids and staff getting sick."

"How about you? Has the water made you sick?"

"No. I live in downtown Prosperino. The water there is fine. Well, so far it is, anyway. My saving grace is that I drink a lot of canned soda instead of water. Not the healthiest thing to do, but in this case my bad habit kept me from drinking the ranch's water and getting sick. Maybe winding up in the hospital."

Using a hand that sported short, unpolished nails, she shoved her long brown hair behind her shoulder. "Blake asked me to bring you back to his office the minute you got here." Turning, she led the way past her desk, Rory following. "I understand you and Blake were roommates in college."

"That's right."

Her mouth curving at the edges, she slid Rory a sideways look. "I bet you could tell me some good stories about Blake."

Rory cocked his head. Although she kept her tone light, he picked up on a personal thread that had him wondering if there was more than just the job between Holly and her boss.

"I could. Problem is, Blake knows some good stories about me, too. I'd better keep my mouth shut."

"I had to try." She gave a brisk tap on a door at the end of the hallway. After a muffled "Come in," she pushed the door open and stepped back for Rory to enter.

"Blake, you have company."

"I'll be damned." Smiling, Blake rose from behind a wide expanse of polished desk and strode across the office. Gripping the hand Rory offered, Hopechest Ranch's director delivered a resounding slap to his friend's shoulder. "How many years has it been?"

"Too many to count."

"I agree."

Blake Fallon had changed little since their college days, Rory decided. His tall, athletic build evidenced the frequent workouts Blake had stuck to when they'd shared a dorm room. The only difference seemed to be that he now wore his dark, thick hair shorter. His skin carried a healthy, golden tan that told Rory his friend didn't spend all of his time behind the neat-as-a-pin desk where a single file folder lay open.

Rory inclined his head toward the desk. "I see you're still chronically neat, Fallon. You still polish your stapler every day?"

Blake chuckled. "At least I can *find* my stapler. I bet you still keep a desk that looks like an avalanche hit it."

"Some things never change."

Out of the corner of his eye, Rory noted that Holly's gaze lingered on her boss for an extra beat before she shifted her attention. "Can I get you some coffee, Mr. Sinclair? Tea?"

"Call me Rory, and I'll pass. I had breakfast before I left the inn."

"Let me know if you change your mind. How about you, Blake?"

"Nothing for me, Holly. I'll let you know if we need anything."

Rory waited until the door clicked shut on Holly's departing form. "Did you tell her I'm FBI?"

"No. You and I are the only ones who know. Until we get to the bottom of things around here, I figured that was best." All of a sudden, Blake's voice sounded deathly tired.

Rory glanced at the office's far corner where two green leather wing chairs and a matching sofa angled around a low coffee table. "We going to stand the whole time I'm here, or are you going to offer me a place to sit?"

Blake shoved a hand through his dark hair then gestured Rory toward the grouping of furniture. "Sorry. My hosting skills are a little off. I didn't get much sleep last night."

"More than just last night, I'd say," Rory observed as he pulled off his leather jacket and tossed it over one of the visitors' chairs that sat in front of the desk. The strain his friend felt showed in the dark circles under his eyes. "You look the same way you did during finals when we crammed a full semester of textbook reading into one week."

"That, in addition to working in a date or two," Blake added as he and Rory settled into wing chairs.

"Those were the days."

Focusing his thoughts on business, Rory rested one ankle on the opposite knee as he leaned back in the chair's leathery softness. "On the phone you gave me an overview of what's happened over the past weeks. I need you to start at the beginning and fill in the details."

"It all seems like a bad dream." As he spoke, Blake rubbed a palm over his face. "Like I told you, back in late November a litter of kittens was born dead. A while later another barn cat and a dog dropped dead on the same day. The dog was old, he'd been around for years, so everyone thought it was age that got him. The cat was only about a year old. Neither did it show signs it'd gotten into a fight, no cuts, wounds or anything. One morning it was chasing mice in the stables, that afternoon it was dead. The ranch foreman found it and buried it. He told me he figured the cat had gotten hold of a mouse that carried some disease or had been poisoned, and that's what killed it."

"Sounds like a logical assumption."

"Yeah. Shortly after that, two kids woke up sick. They're both younger, smaller in build. They bunk next to each other in the building we call The Homestead. It's a dormitory-style lodge where our temporary residents awaiting fostering or adoption stay. Both kids had the same symptoms—headache, vomiting, high fever, muscle aches, disorientation. It was winter, so we'd assumed they'd come down with the flu. At first, the doctor who treated them thought that, too."

"I want to talk to that doctor about the symptoms. What's his name?"

"Jason Colton. He's a GP. His office is across the street from Prosperino Medical Center. I'll give him a call and set up a time for you to see him."

"Good." Rory lifted a brow. "He any relation to the foster family you lived with after your parents split up?"

"Good memory, pal."

"Comes in handy in my job."

"Joe and Meredith Colton are the doc's aunt and uncle."

Rory nodded. "After those first two kids, how long did it take others to start getting sick?"

Blake furrowed his brow. "Not long. They all lived in The Homestead. The floors used there for the sleeping areas are all open and lined with bunk beds. The living room, dining room and kitchen are communal, so everyone intermingles."

"I take it you thought the flu was spreading fast, like it always does."

"Yes. A couple of the counselors got sick, too." As he spoke, Blake knocked a fist lightly against the chair's arm. "I should have figured out the connection to the water sooner."

"The doctor thought it was the flu. From the sound of things, everyone else did, too. I don't know why you should have thought any different."

"I'm director of Hopechest Ranch. That makes me responsible for everyone who steps foot on this property."

"That's a big responsibility for one man to shoulder."

"Yeah." Blake blew out a breath. "Anyway, after

about a week, it dawned on me that the only people getting sick were those who live or work on Hopechest Ranch. Some of my employees live in downtown Prosperino, others on the Crooked Arrow Indian Reservation, which borders the ranch's land. Some of the staff who live here drive into downtown daily to buy supplies. It kept nagging at me that if a rampaging flu was what was making the ranch's people sick, surely it would have spread to the town or the res.''

"One would think.''

"So, since only the people here were sick, it stood to reason that the cause was something on the ranch. I thought maybe it could be low levels of carbon monoxide poisoning from a faulty heater in one of the lodges. E-coli from contaminated meat. Anthrax. Asbestos. I considered everything but the water.''

"Why?''

"We test it. The last time was two days before the dog and the kittens died. Everything checked out.''

"So, if the contamination was intentional, that gives us close to an exact date when it occurred.'' Rory pursed his lips. "What about your water pump? What sort of filter do you have?''

"A gas chlorine injector.''

"So, even if whatever got into the water had a distinctive odor or taste, the injector would have masked that.''

"For a while, anyway. But this stuff is odorless *and* tasteless. Otherwise, with the number of people we've got around here, someone would have noticed a difference in the water.'' Blake leaned forward, propped his elbows on his knees and stared at the floor. "One

morning, I got a call from a counselor at Emily's
House—that's our dorm for unwed mothers. Five of
the girls had woken up deathly ill. One was having
premature labor pains. Doc Colton admitted all of them
to the hospital for tests. At that point, I knew time was
running out. I couldn't wait around until someone died
before I got to the bottom of this. I called the health
department and the EPA.''

"What happened after that?"

"The health department tested all the food, the heat-
ers and the air inside all the facilities, everything.
While they did that, Charlie O'Connell showed up and
checked the water. Bingo, we had the source of contamination. I shut down the well. Since then, I've had
water trucked onto the ranch." Blake stared down at
his hands dangling between his thighs. "You meet up
yet with O'Connell?"

"A couple of times."

"What's your impression?"

"That his favorite pastime is putting the moves on
my landlady." Rory's brows drew together, the annoy-
ance self-directed that the comment had been the first
thought to pop into his head. It sure as hell wasn't what
Blake needed to know.

His friend's brows lifted. "O'Connell making any
progress?"

"Mrs. Honeywell has threatened to toss him and his
belongings out in the street."

"Good for Peggy."

"Yeah." Shifting in his chair, Rory heard again the
edge that had settled in her voice, pictured the heat of
temper that had sparked in those compelling green eyes

when she laid down the law to O'Connell. Dangerous territory, Rory cautioned himself before steering the conversation back to business. "I talked to O'Connell for a couple of minutes this morning about the ranch's water."

"He give you any information?"

"Only that the bacteria that causes cholera isn't what put your people in the hospital."

Blake blinked. "Holy hell, I never thought of cholera."

"Don't, because the EPA has ruled it out. They've probably ruled out other things, too, but O'Connell isn't forthcoming. The bottom line is, he isn't happy about your hiring a private consultant to do the same testing he's doing."

"Too bad. I can't shake the feeling he's up to something. And that something doesn't concern the well-being of Hopechest Ranch or its people."

"You mentioned on the phone you caught O'Connell having some sort of clandestine meetings at one of the ranch's hay sheds."

"Right, it was late evening when I drove by and saw his rented car parked there."

"You didn't get a look at who he was with?"

"All I saw was the rear of their car. It was white."

"Maybe he met a woman there," Rory pointed out. "O'Connell could have been enjoying a literal roll in the hay."

"Possible."

"Since he isn't inclined to share information, I'll have to run duplicate tests that he's already had the EPA's lab run. That'll take time."

"Dammit, Rory, we may not have time." Blake clenched his hands into fists. "If someone purposely contaminated the ranch's water, they might have done it to get back at me, at my family. God knows what the hell they might do next."

Rory's thoughts went back to what Peggy had said in the kitchen that morning when she discovered he knew nothing about the trouble that had befallen Blake the previous year. *I thought you and Blake were friends.*

The echo of her words, and the angry frustration he now saw in his friend's face, had guilt balling in Rory's throat. If he had been any kind of friend to Blake, he would already know what that trouble was.

Setting his jaw, Rory shifted his gaze to the far side of the office where a bookcase sat, its shelves lined with obsessively neat rows of leather volumes. Over the years, there had been many times when he could have phoned Blake, just to say hello. Should have phoned him. Rory hadn't, not once. After all, he was a man who shrugged off relationships. He didn't like maintaining ties. He always felt it was pointless to look back toward the past or to give much thought to the future. He lived for the moment. The now.

For the first time in his life, Rory felt the sharp blade of regret for having taken for granted the closest friendship he'd ever had. "I'm sorry, Blake," he said quietly. "I don't know what happened to you or your family. Or the reason someone might have to get back at you."

Blake rose, moved to the nearest window and stared out. "We haven't exactly kept in touch, have we?"

"My fault," Rory said. "I always put the job first."

Blake slid him a look across his shoulder. "Thanks to your dad, you never learned how to do anything else."

"True." Rory eased out a breath. Blake was one of the few people who knew the history between him and his late father. It was a history that Rory had no desire to discuss.

"Look, we're not talking about me right now. If you think someone contaminated the water on this ranch as revenge against you, I need to know about it. Everything."

Blake ran a palm across the back of his neck. "Christ, you'd think with time, this would get easier to talk about."

"Some things never get easy."

"This is one of them." With a restless move of his shoulders, Blake walked back to his chair. "My dad's gone through three wives—my mother, and the other two left him because of his drinking. I've got three stepsisters I barely know because we all got shuffled from household to household while we were growing up."

Blake paused, as if collecting his thoughts. Rory waited in silence.

"I don't know if I ever told you any of this, but my dad served in the army with Joe Colton. After their discharge, they went to Wyoming where Joe started Colton Mining. A couple of years after that, Joe branched into oil. Later on, shipping. Dad always considered himself Joe's equal partner, but that's not the way things were. Joe's brother, Graham, was his legal partner in Colton Enterprises."

"I take it your dad resented that?"

"Yes. Even when I was little, he felt that Joe and Graham had cheated him out of what was rightfully his. That made him drink more. When my parents' marriage started falling apart, they fought and screamed at each other constantly. Home became a war zone."

"With you in the middle," Rory added.

"Right. I still don't know how, but Joe and Meredith Colton figured out what was going on. They insisted I move in with them at Hacienda de Alegria, their ranch in Prosperino. If they hadn't done that, I would have eventually run off and never come back." Blake shrugged. "Joe took me under his wing, gave me a foundation. He became more of a father to me than Emmett Fallon ever was."

"In college, whenever you mentioned Joe Colton, I got the impression you thought he walked on water."

"I did. Do. Unfortunately, you're not the only one who formed that conclusion. My dad did, too. My going around singing Joe's praises only fed his anger. Last year his drinking got so bad that Joe forced him into retirement. That pushed Dad over the edge. On two separate occasions, he took a shot at Joe. Nearly killed him both times."

"Jesus," Rory said softly. "What happened to Emmett?"

"After evidence against him surfaced, he confessed. Waived a trial and pled guilty. He's at the prison in San Quentin."

"I'm sorry."

"So am I." Blake shook his head. "To the people

in this town, Joe Colton is a saint. My dad's in prison where no one can get to him. The water on Hopechest is contaminated—so far, it's the *only* water around with a problem. What if this is all about my dad trying to kill Joe? What if someone contaminated the water here solely to get back at me?''

''The sins of the father visited on the son?''

''Exactly.''

''Until we know what got into the water and *how* it got there, we can't discount anything.'' Rory furrowed his brow. ''Have you received any threatening letters about what your dad did? Any phone calls?''

''A couple of calls.''

''Did you report them to the police?''

''No. They came in at night on my private line when I was upstairs in bed. The caller didn't actually threaten me, just railed against Dad and called him names. I figured a few people needed to blow off steam.''

''There's always a chance one of those people decided you need to suffer, too.'' Rory tilted his chin. ''What about a family member of Joe's?''

''No. The Coltons bent over backward to help Dad after his arrest. Joe even persuaded the judge to give him a light sentence.''

''Colton does sound a little saintlike.''

''Trust me, he is. He and his wife are paying the cost of all medical expenses for anyone who drank contaminated water.''

Rory expelled a soft whistle. ''That's a lot of money.''

''Right. So, I doubt Joe would have contaminated the water, then turned around and offered to pay everyone's medical expenses. You can cross off everyone close to him, too.''

"Your dad was close to him,'' Rory said quietly. "Sometimes the guilty party is the last person you'd suspect.''

"Yeah. I sure as hell didn't suspect my dad of taking those potshots at Joe.''

"I need a list, Blake. I want the name of every person who stands to profit in any way if you lose your job. I also want the name of anyone who might hold a grudge against you or your family for what Emmett did. That includes all the Coltons, everyone connected with them and the people who might take offense at your father trying to kill Prosperino's favorite citizen.''

"That would be about everyone in town.''

"Doesn't matter. I'll get the list from you later today.'' Rory checked his watch. "I've got my evidence kit in the trunk so I'll take samples from your well before I leave. If possible, I'd like to see Dr. Colton after I'm done here.''

"I'll set it up.'' Blake sat back at his desk.

"Will he balk about releasing copies of toxicology reports on everyone who got sick?''

"No. The kids are legally in the care of Hopechest Ranch so we have access to all their medical information. I'll call Suzanne Jorgenson and have her get the reports. She's one of our counselors who's sitting in on this morning's city council meeting.'' Blake smiled. "Suzanne has a knack for keeping Mayor Longstreet on his toes.''

Blake settled into the chair behind his desk and reached for the phone. In a few minutes, he hung up.

"Jason will be at his clinic all day. His receptionist said for you to just drop by and she'll squeeze you in to see him between patients. Suzanne will get the copies of the tox reports for you and drop them off at Honeywell House."

"Fine."

Leaning back in his chair, Blake gave Rory a tired smile across the expanse of polished desk. "You mentioned you ate breakfast at the inn."

"That's right." Rory retrieved his leather jacket off the chair at the front of the desk. "It is a bed and *breakfast,* you know."

"Do I. Sometimes, when I have an early meeting in town, I drop by Honeywell House first. I always make sure I show up hungry so Peggy will take pity on me and feed me. What did she serve this morning?"

"Pecan pancakes and apple cinnamon sausage." Rory's mouth curved. "I thought I had died and gone to heaven."

"Wait until you taste that apricot cobbler I told you about."

"That'll be tonight."

"Oh, yeah? You already manage to charm the charming Mrs. Honeywell?"

"My charm, although considerable, had nothing to do with it," Rory said dryly as he shrugged on his jacket. "I made a deal—I test the inn's water twice a day, Mrs. Honeywell bakes me a different dessert every night."

"That's some deal." Blake's smile faded. "So, how is the inn's water?"

"Fine. No problems."

"I hope we'll be saying that soon about the ranch's water. Then we can all go back to our own lives."

"Let's hope."

Rory slid his hands into the pockets of his jacket, fisted them. Once he identified what had contaminated the water, he would leave Prosperino, as he had left dozens of other places, hundreds of other people, and go on to the next.

That just the thought of leaving tightened his gut was something he filed away to think about later.

Four

"**I** hope he'll make a difference."

Peggy glanced at Suzanne Jorgenson who sat sipping tea across the small polished span of the table in the alcove just off the kitchen. "Who?"

"Your scientist."

"Mr. Sinclair is your boss's scientist. Blake hired him." As she spoke, Peggy used her gardening shears to snip off the end of an iris stalk. Earlier, she had decided to treat her guests to a touch of spring on this gloomy January afternoon. She had headed to the greenhouse she'd had built on one side of the inn's parking lot and clipped stalks from the bulbs she forced year-round. Now the lush green stalks sporting purple and pink blooms lay like colorful blobs of paint on the newspapers spread across the table.

"Right, Blake's scientist." Violet eyes shadowed by

fatigue met Peggy's gaze over the rim of the teacup. "I'm keeping my fingers crossed that he can figure out what contaminated the ranch's water." Replacing the teacup on its saucer, Suzanne settled a palm on the manila envelope that contained the toxicology reports Blake had asked her to pick up and deliver to Honeywell House. "Watching so many of the kids get sick, then some of the other counselors and staff members has been a nightmare." She shook her head. "Jason Colton still has two of our pregnant teens under observation until he knows for sure what they consumed in the water. Let's hope Sinclair figures it out fast."

"Let's hope." Peggy knew that Rory would immediately check out after he identified the contaminant. Leave Prosperino. She would never again be forced to gaze up into those extraordinary blue eyes while her heart pounded against her ribs. Never feel his long, firm fingers tangle with hers when he helped her to her feet. Never have to stand inches from him while a single, mesmerizing word rolled off his tongue. *Ireland.*

She had never known one word could sound like that—soft and smooth and vaguely exotic. A part of her yearned to wallow in the silky feel of it. Another part cautioned her to keep her distance.

The jolting pleasure at hearing him voice that one word had been followed by a flash of heat that had shocked her by its intensity. She knew that kind of reaction, the depth and suddenness of it, held its own special danger. She had felt that same instant, flash-fire pull to Jay. Then, she had been unable to resist the attraction, powerless to fight it.

She knew, with every instinct she possessed, that if

she didn't keep her distance from Rory Sinclair, she would find herself helplessly drawn in by the aura of danger she sensed in him. The thought allured, and at the same time scared the hell out of her.

"Peggy?"

Her gaze whipped up to meet Suzanne's. "I... What?"

"Something wrong?"

"No." Clearing her throat, Peggy forced back images of the man who had consumed her thoughts since he'd walked into her life the previous night. She had to stop fantasizing over Rory Sinclair. She *had* to.

"I'm sorry, Suzanne, I'm a little distracted. What did you say?"

Her friend pursed her mouth as she watched Peggy stab two iris stalks into a cut-glass vase. "I said, at today's city council meeting, Longstreet announced again that Prosperino's water supply is safe. Says he's sure of that because it's being tested twice a day. The mayor had a couple of pitchers of ice water on the dais that he said came right from the tap. During the meeting, he and the council members all drank their fair share."

"I don't suppose that will stop people from stocking up on bottled water."

"I agree. I think Longstreet is worried that history will repeat itself. Last week, when the delivery of bottled water was late getting to the grocery store, the police had a near riot on their hands."

"I heard." As she spoke, Peggy slid the last of the iris stems into the vase. The arrangement needed some sprigs of her homegrown baby's breath as a finishing touch, she decided. "I won't miss having to stand in the line at the store to buy my ration of bottled water."

"You decide to put all your faith in Prosperino's water testing abilities?"

"That, and Mr. Sinclair's. He's agreed to test the inn's water twice a day."

"Must be nice to have your own private chemist."

"He's not *my* chemist," Peggy blurted, then snapped her jaw shut. Suzanne hadn't meant anything by the remark, yet for reasons Peggy didn't want to acknowledge, she'd found it necessary to make instant denials about her relationship with Rory. *There is no relationship!*

With embarrassment forming a hot ball in her stomach, Peggy met her friend's gaze. "But you're right, it is reassuring to have the inn's water tested daily."

Arching a dark brow, Suzanne leaned in. "Okay, Peg, spill it. What's going on between you and the chemist?"

"Nothing. He just... Nothing."

"Uh-huh."

Peggy laid the shears aside. "He just...he reminds me of Jay, is all."

"You mean, Sinclair looks like Jay?"

"No. I mean Rory...Mr. Sinclair resembles the cop side of Jay."

"Cop side?"

"He's observant. It's like he takes in everything in one look and instantly sizes up a situation."

"Think he might just be a scientist with the eyes of a microscope?"

"It's more than that. He moves like a shadow.

Soundless. Last night I didn't hear a thing when he came through the front door—not even his footsteps on the wood floor. I had no idea he was in the foyer until I turned around and saw him. Jay had that same stealthy way about him.''

Suzanne tilted her head. "Does it upset you to be around a man who reminds you of your husband?''

"No. Jay's been gone nearly five years. It's easier now to focus on all the good times we shared.''

Silently, Peggy conceded that what having Rory around *did* do was make her feel nervous, unsettled and far more interested in him than she had a right to be. After all, the possibility still loomed that there was a Mrs. Sinclair waiting for him in D.C.

Frowning, Peggy sat the cut-glass vase aside, then rolled up the newspapers that held the pieces of stem she'd clipped. "I guess all the worrying over the water is getting to me. I don't know how many hours of sleep I've lost while I've agonized over whether I should take Samantha someplace safe until this crisis is over.''

"I think everyone in town has lost sleep over the water.'' Suzanne rose, carried her cup and saucer to the sink. There, she turned and gazed at the crayon drawings attached by magnets to the refrigerator door. "Speaking of Samantha, how is she?''

"Wonderful.'' Peggy smiled as she dumped the newspaper in the trash, then carried the flower arrangement to the center work island. "Of course, I'm prejudiced.''

"That's a mother's right.'' Suzanne moved to the refrigerator, slid a fingertip along the edge of one of the drawings. "You can't always know where a safe place is for your child, can you? Until two weeks ago Hopechest Ranch fell into that category. Overnight its water supply turned into an environmental nightmare.''

"True." Peggy paused. She saw worry and concern in Suzanne's eyes...and a wistfulness she'd never before seen. "Is something wrong? I mean, other than what you and everyone else who works at Hopechest are having to deal with?''

Suzanne opened her mouth, then closed it. Shaking her head, she retrieved the multicolored wool jacket she'd hung on the coatrack by the back door. "I've got a lot on my mind. A couple of things to figure out. Plus, all those hours I've spent with our two pregnant teens are catching up with me. My brain is toast."

Peggy retrieved her shears off the table, then joined her friend at the door. "You'll let me know if I can help?"

"Sure." Smiling, Suzanne squeezed Peggy's arm. "Thanks for the tea."

"Anytime. I'll walk you out. I need to get some baby's breath from the greenhouse."

The women stepped onto the back porch into the fog-enshrouded afternoon. The rumble of the surf at the base of the nearby cliffs permeated the thick, humid air. Beyond the porch lay the gravel lot. Peggy could barely make out the outline of her black station wagon, which, other than Suzanne's, was the only vehicle parked there.

When she found herself wondering when Rory would return, Peggy tightened her grip on the shears. It wasn't any of her business when he would get back. Didn't matter if he *ever* returned.

Suzanne shoved her hands into the pockets of her jacket while she shot a disparaging look at the gray, overcast sky. "Whoever dubbed this 'sunny California' must have been smoking something at the time."

Laughing, Peggy watched her friend descend the porch steps. "You're right. Come to think of it, we haven't seen the sun for a week. Maybe longer."

"I guess the mood of the town matches the weather these days," Suzanne observed. When she turned to look back up at Peggy, the wind whipped through her dark hair. "Are you bringing Samantha to the arts festival tomorrow night?"

"Definitely. She's been talking for days about her and Gracie making a return visit to the face painting booth. Samantha would never forgive me if we missed the festival."

"See you there, then." Suzanne walked the few steps to her car, slid in, then started the engine.

Peggy lingered on the porch, snipping off several wilted sprigs from the pots of orange and yellow mums that lined the rail. Satisfied, she descended the steps, gravel crunching beneath her shoes as she traversed the parking lot. With each step, the wind whipped at the red velvet ribbon that tied her hair loosely back.

The unremitting gray clouds that blocked the sun transformed the interior of the greenhouse into a dim space where the smell of damp earth mixed with the scent of delicate blooms. Wooden, waist-high potting benches lined both sides of the greenhouse and the wall opposite the door. That bench held empty pots, packets of seeds, a long-spouted watering can and hand tools.

Large bags of peat moss and potting soil shared space in a shadowy corner beside the bench.

The wind battered against the structure's walls and roof, rattling the glass panes. Beneath her gray sweater and slacks, Peggy's skin prickled from the wind's mournful howl and a sensation she couldn't identify.

Another presence? Immediately she dismissed the unsettling thought as her gaze raked the dim, tidy interior, taking in the colorful irises that burst from bulbs planted beside pots of delicate baby's breath and pink tulips. The disconcerting sensation that had suddenly descended around her no doubt came from the wind's forlorn moan.

Shaking her head, she moved to the bench that held rows of small peat pots in which she'd sown seeds the previous week. Although she'd glanced at the pots when she was there earlier, she'd been in a hurry to snip the iris stems and get back to the kitchen to take her sourdough bread out of the oven before it burned. Now that all the baking and cleaning were done for the day—and poor Bugs's head was stitched back on—she lingered over the peat pots, examining the tender sprouts that had just begun to push through the soil.

Peggy's mouth curved with the sense of pleasure she always felt amid the fragrance of loamy earth and delicate blossoms. She could think of few things more intensely satisfying than growing things, giving them life, then watching them flourish in her care.

After a few moments, she glanced at her watch. It was nearly three o'clock. Normally, Samantha would be getting off the bus from preschool about this time. Today, however, was special. Gracie's mom had called and invited Samantha to their house for a session of cookie baking.

Samantha's absence gave Peggy a few extra minutes to linger over her plants. Still, she couldn't get any real work done since it was nearly time to prepare that evening's cheese plate and the accompanying wine to serve her guests in the study.

Turning to the bench opposite the one that held the peat pots, Peggy used the shears to clip a sprig of baby's breath. She had just laid the sprig aside when a vague noise that seemed to come from somewhere behind her sent a chill zipping up her spine. Swallowing hard, she told herself the noise had been nothing more than the wind rattling the panes of glass. Or maybe a car pulling into the parking lot. Those reassuring thoughts didn't stop her from looking across her shoulder while her heart banged against her ribs like a moth against a screen.

The only thing behind her was the bench covered with peat pots. Beyond the glass walls, the fog seemed to have grown more dense. It pressed against the panes, obscuring the parking lot, heightening her sense of isolation.

Turning her attention back to the task at hand, Peggy expelled a slow breath. The half sigh ended in a choked gasp when a hand grabbed her hair in one hard yank that snapped her head back. The pain that stabbed into her skull was like an explosion, as clear as a star on a cold night.

From behind, thick fingers locked like a vise on the back of her neck and lifted. She was nearly on tiptoe, and bent so far backward that her spine threatened to crack.

The strength necessary to raise her almost off her feet told her that her assailant was a man.

She had a sickening half moment to think about rape while she struggled, her body twisting while her blood pounded in her ears. Her hand, still gripping the shears, flailed, stabbing futilely at the air behind her.

Fear screamed through her head, shrieked toward her throat. Before she could make a sound, she was spun toward the rear of the greenhouse then shoved forward. Staggering off-balance, she slammed sideways into the potting bench; the force of the blow sent the shears flying from her grasp. The bolt of pain that exploded in her hip blurred her vision and turned her legs as spindly as a foal's.

She fell hard on her hands and knees to the dirt floor. Dazed, she was vaguely aware of movement behind her, heard the door bang outward, felt the cool wind sweep into the greenhouse's dim recesses. Through a haze of pain and fear, she heard footsteps scrambling across the gravel lot. Then nothing.

He was gone. Had something scared him away? She didn't know. All she knew was that she was alone. Shaking, scared and alone. Until he came back.

Sheer black waves of terror threatened to engulf her. What if he came back? He'd been immensely strong, could have snapped her neck with one twist of his powerful hands. What if he killed her next time? Samantha had no other family, she would be alone. Who would take care of her child? Love her?

Sobbing, Peggy raised a trembling hand above her

head and gripped the edge of the bench. Her fingers slipped, leaving a streak of dirt. She tried again, using both hands. When she pulled herself up, pain seared up and down her thigh from the spot on her hip that had smashed against wood.

Eyes watering from the pain, short breaths scraping at her throat, she took an unsteady step forward. Then another. Her instinct for survival shrieked for her to get inside the inn, get away. Lock herself in before he came back.

Reaching out, she gripped the bench that held the peat pots. She saw that her garden shears had landed in the middle of the small pots, scattering them. Her fingers numb and stiff, she gripped the shears as though they were a weapon. If her attacker came back, if he tried to touch her again, she would use them.

Leaning her weight against the bench, she inched toward the open door, her heart hammering wildly. Fingers of fog crept across the dirt floor, sliding around her ankles like shackles, making her progress seem more of a crawl than an unsteady walk.

Even as she told herself she was more frightened than hurt, her brain registered the sickening crunch of gravel coming from just outside the door.

She went still, her body rigid, every muscle and tendon taut. The fog-obscured silhouette that darkened the doorway sent claws of terror digging into her throat.

He's back.

Panic threatened to swamp her, and she forced it away. She could panic later…if she survived his next attack.

With the quick, instinctive fear of a cornered victim,

she raised the shears. When the dark form advanced through the door, she lunged.

It happened fast, a blur of motion and sound. One second, Rory was striding across the gravel parking lot, his mind half focused on the microbiological quality of Hopechest Ranch's water. The instant he stepped through the door of the greenhouse, adrenaline surged through his chest as he dodged the business end of viciously sharp garden shears.

"What the hell…?"

"Oh, God, it's you. I thought…"

When he saw the shockingly white sheen of Peggy's skin, the pure fear in her moss-green eyes, his heart stopped.

He gripped her shoulders. "What happened?"

"A man grabbed me." She burrowed into Rory's arms as if he were a lifeline. "Did you see him out there?" Her breath came out on a broken sob. "He's out there."

Rory looked toward the door and quelled the urge to go after the guy. With the fog so thick, it would be like searching for someone on a moonless night.

"I didn't see him," Rory said quietly while cursing the fact his gun was upstairs, hidden in his room.

Sliding his arms tighter around Peggy's trembling body, he swept his gaze across the greenhouse's dim interior. Nothing. He saw nothing amiss, except the small pots with tiny green sprouts scattered across one of the wooden benches.

"Are you hurt?"

"Not really."

"Tell me what happened."

She shuddered. "I...thought someone...was behind me. No one was. Then...he grabbed my hair. The back of my neck." Against his chest, Rory felt her hands fist. "He nearly lifted me off the floor. I thought... Oh, God, I thought he was going to..."

Setting his jaw, Rory eased her back. Her sweater was buttoned to the neck, and the only damage to her slacks were smudges of dirt on both knees. If she'd been raped in this setting, her clothing would be soiled, torn.

"I've got you." He closed his eyes, slicked his palm down the length of her ponytail and chose to ignore the hard, jerky beat of his own heart. "He can't hurt you now."

"Samantha. All I could think about was Samantha. How alone she'd be if I died."

Rory's chin jerked up. Dammit, for the first time in his life he'd broken one of the ironclad rules of being a cop. He had let himself feel instead of think. Less than five minutes ago, he'd parked his rental car in the lot, gone into the inn through the front door and immediately started looking for Peggy. When he got to the kitchen, he spotted the flowers in the vase. Since her station wagon was parked outside, he figured she was around somewhere, so he took a chance she might be in the greenhouse. During his short time indoors, he hadn't heard or seen Samantha.

The thought that some scum had attacked the mother to buy time to snatch her child put a sick feeling in Rory's gut. He'd worked enough crime scenes that involved kidnapped children to last a lifetime. Swallowing hard, he forced his voice to remain steady. "Where's Samantha?"

"At a friend's house."

Relief rose in him like a wave. "Do you know who attacked you?"

"I...never saw his face."

"Did he use a weapon?"

"Just his hands." Her voice quavered. "They were enough."

"Okay." Nudging her gently back a step, Rory peeled off his leather jacket, settled it over her shoulders. "I'm taking you inside, Ireland." In an unconscious gesture, he skimmed his long fingers over her pale cheek. Even her lips had lost color. "You need to lie down while I call the police."

"I... Fine."

They started toward the door. With his arm draped around her thin waist, Rory not only saw but felt the limp in her walk. His eyes narrowed as he halted.

"You are hurt." That knowledge sent fury pounding through him.

"He shoved me." When she looked up, he saw a flash of pain in her green eyes. "My hip rammed into the potting bench."

"The son of a bitch." Teeth set, Rory tightened his arm around her waist. "I'm also calling a doctor."

"My hip's bruised, is all. I don't need a doctor."

"Why don't we let someone with the letters M.D. after their name confirm that?"

"I don't need a doctor. Really." She ran her tongue over her lips. "Some tea, a couple of aspirin, a hot bath and I'll be fine."

When she leaned into him, Rory felt something move inside him. Something he was at a loss to identify. "I'll make sure you get all of those things," he said quietly. "Plus a session with a doctor." Never before had he felt such a searing need to protect. To rescue.

"I'm fine." She was shaking like a leaf. "I just…need to get off my feet for a minute," she said, then closed her eyes.

"I can help you there, too, Ireland."

Sweeping her into his arms, Rory carried her out into the fog and the wind.

Five

"You can set me down at the table," Peggy said when Rory shouldered open the back door and stepped into the kitchen. She knew her voice still sounded shaky. She couldn't help it.

"You need to lie down." With her tucked firmly in his arms, he used one foot to shove the door closed behind them. "Where's your room?"

"I just need to sit—"

"Through there?" he asked, inclining his head toward a dim hallway that jutted off the back of the kitchen.

She raised a hand, intent on protesting. When she realized she was still trembling from the attack, she expelled an unsteady breath. Maybe she did need a little more comfort than what a kitchen chair had to offer.

"Yes, through there."

He carried her effortlessly down the hallway, then through the open door into the sitting room painted in soft white where a forest-green, button-tufted couch and matching chairs grouped around a low coffee table. Bugs, his pink fur looking worn and matted, lay on the table. After she'd stitched the poor rabbit's head back on, Peggy had looped a length of white gauze around his neck, tourniquet-style.

Rory paused, his gaze flicking between the two closed doors at the rear of the room. "Which is your bedroom?"

The thought of him venturing into the intimate confines of her bedroom tightened Peggy's throat. "Just put me on the couch."

"You need to lie down."

"I will. On the couch."

When he hesitated, she pressed her palm against his chest and attempted to push from his arms. The feel of rock-hard muscles beneath her fingers told her she would have as much luck trying to move a brick wall.

His arms tightened around her. "Okay, the couch," he said, turning on his heel.

He leaned, settling her gently into a V of soft cushions and throw pillows at one end of the couch. The gesture put his nose, his eyes, his mouth even with hers. Although she was still feeling the effects of the attack, that didn't prevent her heart from flipping straight into her throat and blocking any chance of air.

When her breath hitched, his blue eyes narrowed. "You okay, Ireland?"

Her lips parted. If he leaned the slightest bit forward,

his mouth would be on hers. His eyes had flecks of aquamarine in them that she hadn't noticed before. His tangy scent rose from his leather jacket that still covered her shoulders. The clean, salty smell of his skin seeped into her lungs, reminding her what it was like to be this close to a man. It had been so long, so very long, since she'd been held. Just held.

"I'm fine." Her voice wavered as she tried to ignore the ache in her throat where her pulse had begun to pound. "I'm…a little shaky."

His gaze dropped to her throat, lingered there. With quiet deliberation, he lifted his eyes to hers. Their lethal blue color had gone one shade darker. "So am I." He cupped his hand to her cheek too gently for her to refuse the contact. "Right now, I need to call the police. If the guy is still anywhere near, the cops might get lucky and pick him up."

"True."

When he straightened and headed across the room for the phone that sat on the small writing desk tucked into a corner, Peggy raised a hand to her throat. Her pulse hammered madly beneath her fingertips. If he hadn't moved when he did, she knew she would have started shaking like a leaf again.

Not from fear this time. Any question about whether Rory was as attracted to her as she was to him had been answered when his gaze lifted to hers and she'd glimpsed raw need in his eyes.

Nothing could come from that attraction, she reminded herself while she worried her bottom lip between her teeth. She wouldn't let it. Even if Rory wasn't married—which he might be—he was just passing through. He could be packed and gone within a week, maybe even a few days.

"I need to report an assault."

The cold reality of the words Rory spoke into the phone focused her thoughts. She gripped one of the throw pillows that littered the couch and pulled it against her chest. Jay had died one week after she found out she was pregnant, yet she had not felt as vulnerable then as she did right now. Someone had attacked her, could have done unspeakable things to her. Killed her. Her emotions were roiling, her senses reeling. She was simply having a natural reaction that made a part of her want to cling to the man who had swept her into his arms and carried her to safety.

She had to get her balance back. *Intended* to get it back. She had an inn to operate and a daughter to take care of. She was going to report what had happened to the police and later, soak in a hot bath to ease the stiffness that had already settled into her hip. She had never treated intimacy casually and she was *not* going to get involved with a man she barely knew whose long, narrow face looked akin to a pirate's.

"Dispatch is sending a uniform by."

"Good." Her eyes narrowed. "You sound like a cop."

"Just repeating what the dispatcher told me." As he spoke, Rory slid his fingertips into the back pocket of his black jeans and pulled out a business card. "I need to make another call. After that, I'll bring you some tea and a couple of aspirins."

"Thanks."

He checked the card, then punched a number into

the phone. "This is Rory Sinclair, I was there a couple of hours ago. It's important that I speak with Dr. Colton again. Yes, *now.*"

Peggy ignored the pain that jabbed in her hip when she leaned forward. "I told you, I'm fine. A little bruised and stiff, is all. There's no need to bother Jason."

Rory flicked her a look out of the corner of his eye, then turned his back on her and began talking into the phone.

Eyebrows knitted, she tugged his leather jacket off her shoulders, laid it across the top of the couch then leaned back. That was the problem, she reasoned. The instant she'd seen him standing in the foyer last night, watching in silence while she put that lech, O'Connell, in his place, she had sensed that Rory Sinclair always did exactly what he pleased. He was tough and authoritative, a man whom a woman would be helpless to guide...or control.

That, she thought on a sigh, was what made him so dangerously appealing.

"So, you never saw his face?" Sergeant Kade Lummus asked a half hour later from the chair nearest the couch on which Peggy sat. "Not even a glimpse?"

"No. Like I said, he stayed behind me with one of his hands in my hair, the other locked on the back of my neck. The only way I'm sure it was a man was because of his strength. For an instant, he nearly lifted me off my feet."

When the sergeant arrived, Rory had settled on the end of the couch opposite Peggy. From there, he had answered the few questions Lummus had directed at him, then spent the remainder of the interview quietly observing. Lummus was in his mid-thirties, tall, with a tough, sinewy look about him. His uniform was pressed, the creases in his dark pants sharp enough to shave ice. He had a shrewd, intelligent face, thick black hair and observant brown eyes. It hadn't been lost on Rory that, the instant Lummus strode into Peggy's small living room, those eyes had filled with concern that went way past professional.

Crossing his arms over his chest, Rory shifted his gaze from Lummus to the opposite end of the couch. Sometime during the interview, Peggy had untied the bloodred ribbon that had held her hair loosely back. Now dark waves framed her face, tumbling down over the shoulders of her gray sweater. Her skin, which had looked sickly pale right after the attack, had regained its ivory creaminess.

He couldn't ignore the fact that he liked looking at her. Any more than he could shrug off the kick of lust he'd felt when he'd settled her on the couch and his mouth had wound up an inch from hers. Or the need that had clawed inside him when he saw her pulse pounding wildly in her throat.

Pounding for him.

He had known, in that split-second of time, that he could have her.

The memory had Rory rubbing a hand across his face. It had been more than just the knowledge of how vulnerable the attack had left her that had made him take a step back. It was the realization that there was more involved. Something that went beyond the physical. Admiration, he decided. How could he not admire a woman armed only with garden shears who had the mettle to lunge at a man? A tightness settled in his chest as he pictured her with weapon raised and fire in her green eyes. Yes, whatever it was that had his insides knotted went way beyond physical.

And he damn well didn't like it. Any more than he liked the feeling of restless discontent that had plagued him over the last couple of months. Once his job in Prosperino was done, he would call his supervisor, extend his leave, go off somewhere. He needed some quiet time to think, to logic out what the hell it was in his life that had changed. Then fix it.

"I should have done something to protect myself," Peggy snapped at Lummus. "I took that self-defense class last year that you recommended. In the greenhouse, my brain locked up and I couldn't remember a thing. That shouldn't have happened."

Focusing back on the interview, Rory conceded that Peggy's reaction was normal. Enough time had passed since the attack that her fear had turned to anger.

Lummus apparently recognized that, too, since he nodded and said, "A woman trying to defend herself against a man twice her size doesn't have a lot of options. Like you told me, the guy was big. Strong. You couldn't exactly wrestle him to the ground."

"I should have done *something*. I didn't even scream." Peggy's voice quavered. Pressing her lips together, she looked down at her lap where her fingers had a death grip on a throw pillow.

Rory leaned forward, forcing her to meet his gaze. "You did do something. You survived." His mouth curved. "And when you thought the creep had come back, you nearly put out one of my eyes with your garden shears."

She nodded, pulled in a deep breath. "Maybe I did do okay."

Lummus rose. "You did more than okay." He slid the small pad on which he'd been jotting notes back into his uniform shirt pocket. "I need to get this information on the air. We've had a couple of reports over the past week of a transient hanging around in the area. This could be the guy who attacked you. Maybe he hid in your greenhouse to get out of the cold and fog."

"That doesn't explain why he attacked me."

Lummus gazed down at her, his eyes concerned and intense. "The only place he could have hidden was under one of the potting benches. Maybe he figured it was only a matter of time before you spotted him. You had those shears. Could be he decided to go on the defensive and attack while you still didn't know he was there." The cop shrugged. "My guess is you scared him as bad as he scared you. He could be in the next county by now."

Peggy sent him a weak smile. "I hope you're right, Kade."

Rising, Rory snagged her empty teacup from off the table. "How about more tea while you're waiting for the doctor to arrive?"

She scowled. "How about you call Jason and tell him not to waste his time coming here?"

"How about I get you more tea?"

Lummus stepped to the couch, paused, then settled

a hand on her shoulder. "Peggy, it won't hurt for Jason to have a look at you," he said quietly.

She smiled up at him. "Thanks, Kade. I appreciate you getting here so fast."

When she placed a hand on the cop's, a surge of emotion—feeling dangerously like jealousy—hit Rory in the center of his chest. Tightening his grip on the cup, he turned and walked down the short hallway, then into the kitchen.

With the late afternoon quickly transforming to evening, he flicked on the light switch. The copper pots suspended from the rack over the center island glowed in the instant illumination from the overhead lights.

It wasn't the warm scent of baking that permeated the air, he realized. The whole room smelled like Peggy, that hot, spicy scent that made a man's mouth water.

"You're in big trouble, Sinclair," he muttered.

Shaking his head, he sat the cup on the island beside the paper sack he had lain there earlier that afternoon when he'd arrived back at the inn. The item in the sack was the reason he had ventured out to the greenhouse in search of Peggy.

When Lummus strode into view, Rory forced back the notion that the cop had lingered down the hall because he'd put a liplock on the inn's proprietress. Some thoughts were better ignored.

"Do you really have reports of a transient in the area?" Rory asked.

Lummus flicked him a look while shrugging on his quilted uniform jacket. "Two reports. Both from last week." He glanced back at the hallway, then remet

Rory's gaze. "Both sightings occurred on the other side of Prosperino. Still, the guy could have made his way to this part of town by now."

"Could have." Rory leaned a hip against the counter. "Your theory of a transient makes sense when you take into account that the attack occurred in a greenhouse. We know for sure the guy was there before Mrs. Honeywell went inside, otherwise she'd have heard him come in. There's nothing in there worth stealing, so it wasn't someone looking for loot to pawn."

Lummus angled his head. "You said you're a chemist, here working for Blake Fallon. Checking out the water at Hopechest Ranch."

"That's right."

"You mix in some law enforcement training with that science degree, Sinclair?"

Rory smiled. He figured Lummus would call Blake to check him out. "Like you said, Sergeant, I'm a chemist. I like to work out solutions to puzzles. I'm puzzled by what the man was doing in the greenhouse. What you said sounds logical." He raised a palm. "It computes."

"Yeah, computes." Lummus glanced back at the hallway, his mouth tightening. "I figure the guy took off because he heard your car drive up. I don't like thinking about what he might have done to Peggy if he'd had more time."

Rory let out a slow breath. "Neither do I."

"How long you planning on staying in Prosperino?"

"Until I get an ID on what contaminated the water

at Hopechest. That could take a few more days, maybe a couple of weeks.''

Lummus reached into the pocket of his jacket, pulled out a business card and handed it to Rory. ''I'd appreciate it if you keep your eyes open while you're here. Call me if anything doesn't seem right or if you spot someone hanging around the inn who doesn't fit. My home number's on the back of the card.''

''Sure.''

Nodding, the cop turned, strode to the door and pulled it open. Rory stared down at the business card while wondering if Peggy knew the guy had a thing for her. Wondering, too, if she had a thing for Lummus.

Footsteps coming from the dining room had Rory turning just as Charlie O'Connell stepped into the kitchen. The EPA inspector was still favoring the ankle he'd twisted during that morning's tumble down the stairs. His tan overcoat was draped over one shoulder.

''What's the patrol car doing outside?'' O'Connell asked.

Rory slid Lummus's card into his back pocket. ''A man attacked Mrs. Honeywell while she was working in her greenhouse.''

''*Attacked* her?'' O'Connell blinked. ''She okay?''

The EPA inspector was wearing the same crimson sweater and khaki slacks he'd had on that morning, Rory noted. He couldn't see any evidence of the greenhouse's dirt floor on the light-colored slacks.

''Shaken up. To be on the safe side, Dr. Colton is coming over to take a look at her.''

''That's probably a good idea.''

Rory angled his chin. "Mind telling me where you were around three o'clock this afternoon?"

O'Connell's mouth tightened. "I take it that's when she got jumped?"

"Yes." Rory raised a shoulder. "No offense. The cop who took the report asked me to check some things out. That's what I'm doing."

"I was at the res."

"Crooked Arrow?"

"Yeah, Crooked Arrow Reservation. There's a new water well being dug there, near where the res borders Hopechest Ranch property. I've been out there before, but I wanted to have another look at that well. Plenty of people saw me."

"In that case, you're in the clear." Although Rory had no real reason to think that O'Connell had been the man who assaulted Peggy, he planned to check his alibi. "Find anything of interest at the well?"

O'Connell's mouth curved. "Remember what I told you this morning, Sinclair? I'm not doing your work for you. You go take a look at that well, then let me know what you find."

Rory shook his head. "Far be it for us to cooperate."

"We aren't cooperating, I keep telling you that." O'Connell glanced around the kitchen, then frowned.

"Something wrong?"

"The two art biddies drove into the parking lot right behind me. They always make a point to be back here in time for wine and cheese in the study, unlike those honeymooners who never show their faces. Peggy always lights the fire and puts on music. I came through the study—no cheese, no fire, no nothing."

Rory lifted a brow. "So you decided to come in here and see why?"

"That's right." O'Connell stuck a hitchhiker-like thumb in the direction of the study. "Between them, those two dames must wear a hundred bracelets. The clacking noise drives me nuts. Checking on this evening's snack was the quickest way for me to get away from them."

More like give yourself another opportunity to hustle the landlady, Rory thought. Sorry, pal, not tonight.

O'Connell shrugged. "I'll go tell them about Peggy's accident and that they should just go on out to dinner."

"No, you don't." If Rory knew anything about Peggy, it was that she prided herself on seeing to the needs of her guests. That she hadn't yet remembered to serve that evening's wine and cheese spoke volumes about how shaken the attack had left her. The minute she remembered, she'd be on her feet, scurrying around. He closed his eyes for a brief instant. He hadn't forgotten how impossibly pale her skin had been, the absolute fear in her eyes. The knowledge of what the bastard could have done to her twisted in Rory's gut.

He blew out a breath, pulled open the door of the refrigerator. "I don't know about you, O'Connell, but I learned a long time ago how to open a package of cheese."

"Guess it doesn't take a rocket scientist," O'Connell observed while Rory pulled open drawers filled with fresh produce and vegetables with such deep color they looked like they were still hanging on the vine.

"Just a mere scientist." Rory snatched two blocks

of plastic-wrapped cheese out of the third drawer he tried. "Grab a plate. And a knife." He nudged the refrigerator door shut with an elbow, moved to the center island. "Where does Mrs. Honeywell keep the wine?"

"There's a rack in the study. Glasses are in a cabinet there."

"Perfect." Rory unwrapped both blocks of cheese then plopped them on the plate O'Connell had pulled out of a cabinet. For the finishing touch, Rory stabbed a knife into the center of one of the blocks. "When you get to the study, pick out a bottle of wine. Serve yourself and the art ladies." As he spoke, Rory shoved the plate into the man's hands. "Have a great happy hour."

O'Connell gave the plate a disparaging look. "Anyone ever tell you that you leave a lot to be desired when it comes to aesthetics, Sinclair?"

"Yeah, and it broke my heart."

"I'll bet," O'Connell muttered as he limped out the door.

Rory checked his watch. It was nearly six. Jason Colton had promised he would drop by the inn after he finished his rounds at the hospital—probably around six-thirty.

"I can't believe I forgot!"

Rory turned in time to see Peggy walk stiffly out of the rear hallway. He scowled. "You're supposed to be on the couch."

"I can't be on the couch," she said as she moved toward the refrigerator. "Not when I have guests to serve."

He reached the refrigerator before she did and leaned

a shoulder against its door where magnets anchored a myriad of crayon drawings. "You don't need to serve your guests."

"Says who?"

"Me."

She lifted her chin. "Look, Sinclair, I've gone after you once today with a sharp implement. Don't make me do it again."

Chuckling, he ran a fingertip down her cheek. "You're tough, Ireland."

"I'm not trying to be tough. I'm trying to operate a business. You're not helping."

"A lot you know. Your guests are already taken care of." He inclined his head in the direction of the study. "They've got a cheese plate. Wine." At that instant, a soft stirring of classical music drifted in on the air. He gave her a self-satisfied grin. "Music. They're fine."

A crease formed between her brows. "You fixed a cheese plate?"

"To tell you the truth, I can't take all the credit. O'Connell helped."

"Are you serious?"

"Totally. He's also in charge of lighting a fire."

"But—"

"No buts." Placing his hands on her shoulders, Rory steered her toward the small table in the alcove just off the kitchen. "Don't act so shocked, Ireland. Some men are perfectly capable of getting around a kitchen."

"And there are some who won't lift a finger and depend on their wives to do everything."

"Well, there is no Mrs. Sinclair. That means I have

to fend for myself. Like unwrapping a hunk of cheese and cutting off a couple of slices. It's not a big deal.''

When he pulled a chair out from the table, she hesitated. "Oh."

"Oh, what?"

"Nothing." She settled stiffly into the chair.

"I still owe you that second cup of tea."

"You don't owe me anything, Mr. Sinclair. In fact, I owe you."

He crossed his arms over his chest. "What exactly do you think you owe me, Mrs. Honeywell?"

"For one thing, my thanks. For rescuing me in the greenhouse. Thank you."

"My pleasure," he said smoothly. "Although, by the time I got there, you didn't need rescuing."

"I also owe you dessert tonight."

Rory stared down at her, saw the shadows beneath her eyes. "I figure you've had a full day already."

"A deal's a deal."

"True." Turning, he walked back to the center island. There, he filled the cup with water, slid in a tea bag, put the cup in the microwave and punched its controls. "Tell you what. I'll trade tonight's dessert for lunch tomorrow."

"Lunch."

"Right. I plan to work in my room most of the day, running preliminary tests on the water samples I collected at Hopechest Ranch."

"Speaking of that." Peggy patted a manila envelope lying beside her on the table. "Suzanne Jorgenson brought this by. She said they're the toxicology reports you asked for."

"Good. Add those to the list of things I need to take a look at tomorrow. With all the work I've got ahead of me, it would be a real inconvenience to have to go somewhere and pick up lunch."

Peggy ran a fingertip across the envelope. "It's a deal, Mr. Sinclair."

"Rory."

"Momma!" Samantha burst through the back door, then swung it shut with a clatter. "Guess what Gracie 'n' me baked?"

Clad in a powder-blue thermal jacket and gripping a paper plate covered with foil, the little girl rushed across the kitchen to her mother's side.

"Gracie and *I*, sweetheart," Peggy said, deftly accepting the plate tilted precariously toward her lap. "Let's see what we've got here."

"It's cookies!" Samantha announced, dancing from foot to foot in anticipation before Peggy had a chance to pull off the foil.

"They look delicious."

"Yeah, they taste real good." Samantha shoved a tumble of dark curls behind one shoulder. "Mrs. Warren let me put the frosting on all by myself."

Rory arched a brow. From where he stood, it looked as if at least an inch-deep glob of chocolate frosting covered the top of each cookie.

"And you did a wonderful job." Smiling, Peggy slid the plate onto the table, then unzipped Samantha's jacket and tugged it off. Rory saw a flicker of pain in Peggy's eyes when Samantha bumped against her hip.

A hard knot formed in his throat. He remembered the desperation in her eyes, the absolute fear in her voice when she'd looked up at him in the greenhouse and said, *Samantha. All I could think about was Samantha. How alone she'd be if I died.*

He knew too well what happened to a child when it lost the only parent who loved them.

"You can have a cookie, too, Mr. Rory."

His chin lifted. Peggy sat at the table, giving him a mild look while taking the first bite from the frosting-laden cookie balanced on her fingertips. Samantha, still clad in the hot-pink romper from that morning, looked at him, eagerness glowing in her dark eyes.

"Just one?"

"Well, one at a time," Samantha said, giving him a stern look.

"Use both hands," Peggy cautioned as her daughter retrieved the paper plate off the table.

Rory walked around the island, crouching when Samantha reached him. "Thanks." He flicked a meaningful look at Peggy. "There's nothing better than having a beautiful woman make me dessert."

Samantha giggled. "I'm not a woman."

"No, but you're a looker."

"What's a looker?"

"You." Rory tweaked her nose, took the plate, then rose and placed it on the island. He selected a hopelessly deformed cookie, then bit it. He blinked as his system absorbed the punch of sugar.

"What's in there?"

He glanced down. Samantha was now standing on sneaker-clad tiptoes, peering over the edge of the counter into the sack he'd carried home from the hospital's gift shop. He had intended to check with Peggy before giving Samantha the gift. Too late now.

"It's a present for you." Reaching into the bag, he pulled out the fuzzy pink rabbit, then stooped down until he and Samantha were eye to eye. "I spotted her in the window of the hospital's gift shop. She looked lonesome. I decided you were the right person to keep her company."

"A new Bugs!" Samantha squealed as she engulfed the rabbit in her arms. "Momma, Mr. Rory bought me a new Bugs!"

Peggy's eyes were warm when they met his. "I see."

"Thank you, Mr. Rory!" Samantha threw herself at him, wrapping a thin arm around his neck. The hug went straight to Rory's heart.

With a stranglehold on the rabbit, Samantha dashed back to Peggy. "Now Bugs has a friend. Her name's Bugsy. Momma, can I take them to the arts festival tomorrow night?"

"I think they'll both fit in your backpack."

"'N Mr. Rory, too?"

With a laugh, Peggy ruffled her daughter's dark curls. "I don't think he'll fit in your backpack."

"I know," Samantha said with exasperation. "Can we take him with us to the festival?"

Peggy looked up, met his gaze. She had a beautifully expressive face. He could read every emotion. He knew without a doubt she was as uneasy as he was about the attraction that drew them like divining rods to water.

"Mr. Sinclair was just telling me about all the work

he has to do tomorrow. I doubt he has time to go to the festival.''

"I'll make time," Rory said quietly. Folded in his pocket was Blake Fallon's list with the names of everyone who stood to gain if he lost his job as director of Hopechest Ranch. On a second list were the names of people who might take revenge on Blake for his father having made two attempts on Joe Colton's life. Not only would attending the festival give Rory a chance to meet some of those people, he would also get a flavor for Prosperino and a lay of the land. That might come in handy later if it turned out someone had purposely contaminated the ranch's water.

"Just let me know what time I need to be ready," he said, then took another bite of cookie. The fact that he found himself anticipating spending more time with the intriguing mother and daughter who currently gazed at him from across the kitchen was something he chose not to examine too closely.

Six

There is no Mrs. Sinclair.

Peggy blew out a breath as she arranged Rory's lunch on a white wicker tray. Her brain had echoed his marital status only about a hundred times since he'd imparted that information last night.

There is no Mrs. Sinclair. That made him single. Eligible. Available. And totally off-limits.

"Totally," Peggy murmured as she hefted the tray and started toward the foyer.

Despite her growing attraction to the man, she knew she had to be practical. An affair with Rory was out of the question. After all, they were from separate worlds. Hers was a Victorian inn perched against a hillside that faced the rugged California coast. His, a sterile laboratory somewhere in Washington, D.C.

Knowing he would return to that lab in the near future should have been the equivalent of a blast of ice water in her face. Instead, a deep, dark ache pulled at her to make the most of the time they had.

She could feel herself blushing as she started up the staircase, favoring her stiff hip. How, she wondered, had it come so far, so fast that just the *thought* of feeling Rory's hands on her flesh could start her heart racing?

She was certain the unsettling events of the previous day were the reason her emotions had veered out of kilter. Rory had swept her to safety, comforted her, tended to her guests. Then there was Samantha. The instant Rory handed her child a fuzzy pink rabbit, Peggy had felt a little crack around her heart.

How could she possibly have a defense against a man like that?

When she reached the door of Rory's third-floor room, she knocked softly and waited. When no response came, a crease formed between her brows. Last night his plan had been to work in his room most of today. He had not come down for breakfast—a fact that'd had Samantha's bottom lip poking out in a pout before she'd left for preschool.

Peggy shook her head at the memory. Her daughter was friendly and outspoken and well-used to being around the inn's guests who arrived and left like clockwork. Still, Peggy had never seen Samantha take to anyone the way she had Rory. That meant she would have to deal with the disappointment that would inevitably accompany his leaving. Making sure Samantha's attachment to him didn't intensify was another good reason for them both to have as little contact with Rory as possible.

As it turned out, he might not even be on the premises, Peggy decided, her arms beginning to ache from the weight of the loaded tray.

Whether Rory's car was still parked in the lot, she didn't know. She hadn't ventured outside that morning—had not yet gotten up the nerve to go anywhere near her greenhouse. If his plans had changed and he had left for a while, she would use the passkey she carried in the pocket of her slacks and take advantage of his absence to change the towels and linens in his room.

She knocked again, more loudly, and still got no response. Shifting the tray, she pulled her key from her pocket, slid it into the lock, then eased the door open.

The bed was unmade, the star-patterned quilt trailing across the brass footboard onto the floor. A pair of khaki pants and a tan sweater lay on top of the tangled sheet and blanket; brown leather loafers sat on the braided rug at the side of the bed.

She stepped over the threshold, then jolted when Rory strode out of the bathroom, wearing nothing but a white towel barely hitched at his hips. His black hair was wet, slicked back from his face in a way that enhanced the strong, smooth line of his jaw. Slowly, her gaze went to the broad chest tanned and darkened by sleek black hair. And those shoulders... Her fingers tightened on the tray.

He met her gaze, his lips curving, slow and deliberate. "It's always nice to find a beautiful woman in my bedroom."

"I'm sorry." How could one man ooze so much charm and sex appeal with just one smile? "I... knocked. Twice. When you didn't answer, I thought you might have left."

He cocked his head, his blue gaze sliding steadily down the length of her black turtleneck and tapered slacks. The way his eyes measured, assessed made Peggy want to squirm.

"How's the hip, Ireland?"

"Better." She took a breath. "Stiff."

"I imagine." He nodded at the wicker tray. "Didn't I hear Dr. Colton tell you to avoid climbing stairs for a couple of days?"

"That's easy for Jason to say. I have guests to attend to. Rooms to clean. I can't do my work if I don't use the stairs."

"Delivering my lunch isn't part of your work," Rory said as he walked to where she stood.

He smelled of subtle, woodsy cologne, with undertones of soap from his shower. Nerves scrambled inside her stomach like crabs on a beach. For one brief instant, there seemed to be only his overwhelming presence in the small room, only *his* compelling scent.

"We made a deal," she managed. "Lunch for dessert."

"The deal was you *make* me lunch. Not deliver it." He nudged the tray from her hands, then turned and carried it to the chest of drawers built of whitewashed pine. "I was just about to come down to the kitchen."

"Not dressed like that, I hope."

The unrepentant grin he shot her over his shoulder

told her he had no problem walking around in front of her wearing only a towel. "Don't like my outfit?"

"Kitchen rules—no shoes, no shirt, no service."

"I'd better get dressed, then." He crossed to the bed, snagged up the khaki pants. "Like I keep telling you, Ireland, you're a tough one."

"And don't forget it." If she was so tough, why were her palms sweating? She rubbed them down her thighs and diverted her gaze from the broad expanse of his bare chest.

On the desk opposite the bed sat a small computer amid vials of what appeared to be water propped upright in a metal rack. Several file folders lay open beside the computer. On the floor sat a printer, churning out pages.

"You're working. And I have to get back to—"

"Give me a minute," he said, then headed across the room. "I need to ask you a question," he added, before disappearing into the bathroom.

Peggy closed her eyes and made a concerted effort not to try to imagine what he looked like beneath that towel.

Seconds later he appeared around the door. "I worked most of the night, running tests on the water samples I took from Hopechest," he said while hooking the waist button on his khakis. "So I slept in."

She nodded toward the desk. "Having any luck?"

"No." He retrieved his tan sweater off the bed, slid it on, then walked to stand beside her. "I can do basic, preliminary testing using my field kit. About the only things I can check for are waterborne diseases like dysentery, typhoid, polio, hepatitis."

"And?"

"I know the contamination isn't microbial, which includes the diseases I just mentioned and a few other things. I'm also sure the problem isn't from a radioactive substance."

Peggy arched a brow. "That has to be good news."

"It is. The downside is the last two categories the contaminant might be from are the largest. One is organic chemical substances, like pesticides, byproducts of industrial processes and petroleum production. The inorganic category includes salts, metals and numerous other compounds that don't contain carbon."

"If you can't run tests here using your field kit, then where?"

"I need a lab that has a gas chromatograph, mass spectrometer and Simultaneous ICP instrument." He paused, raised a shoulder at her blank expression. "That stands for Inductively Coupled Plasma."

"If you say so," she murmured. The man was giving her a science lesson, and all she could think of was how conscious she was of him, standing there, not more than a few inches away. Even though he'd slipped on his sweater, she was still aware of every muscle, every ridge in that broad, solid chest.

He grinned. "Sorry, the scientist in me got carried away."

"It's okay." She forced her thoughts to a safer area. "It sounds like you know what you're doing, and I'm not sure I can say that about Mr. O'Connell. No one in Prosperino will breathe easy until we know what got into the ranch's water. And how it got there. I hope you find out soon. I also hope you'll stop work long enough to eat your lunch," she added, then started to turn away. "I have to get back to—"

He caught her elbow, turned her back to face him. "You haven't given me a chance to ask my question."

She looked up, met his blue gaze while her throat tightened. What was he doing to her? she wondered. How could he make her feel so many different things in so short a time? She nudged her arm from his hold. "What's the question?"

"I need a lab with the instruments I mentioned."

"I don't have a clue where one would be."

"I do. It's in San Francisco. Problem is, that's over a three-hour drive away. I need to find someone who has a private plane for rent. Do you know anyone around here who fits that bill?"

"Michael Longstreet. He's Prosperino's mayor." She angled her chin. "I don't know if he could get away to fly you, though. He has his hands full dealing with the water problem."

"He doesn't need to fly me. I'm a licensed pilot. Any idea what kind of plane Longstreet has?"

"All I know is it's a small jet."

"Perfect."

Peggy felt a tightness settle in her chest at the possibility of Rory's leaving. "Do you plan to stay full-time in San Francisco while you work at the lab there?"

"No. I have to get everything set up, but the tests run in stages over a couple of days and the results take a while. I need to spend more time here looking at groundwater sources on Hopechest Ranch. There's a new well being drilled on the reservation near the ranch's property line. I want to take a look at that well, too."

"I thought the water on the res tested safe."

"It has." He raised a shoulder. "I just like to look at every piece in a puzzle. If I have a couple of days access to a plane, I can get back here, do what I need to do, then return to San Francisco a couple of times to check on the tests."

"It sounds like you'll need this room a while longer."

"Right." He gazed down at her, his eyes intense. "I still have some things I want to do here."

It couldn't be her imagination that his voice had softened, lowered. Otherwise, why would her nerves have started humming like a plucked harp string?

She moistened her suddenly dry lips. "Samantha will be happy to hear you're staying. Between you and me, she has grand plans to draw you a special picture to thank you for Bugsy."

"Can't wait to see it." When he snagged her hand and curved his long fingers around hers, Peggy's heart stuck in her throat. "What about Samantha's mother? How does she feel about my hanging around awhile longer?"

"It's good for business to have the guest rooms rented."

He tightened his fingers around hers when she tried to draw away. "What are we going to do about this, Ireland?"

"This room?" she asked weakly.

"This attraction," he corrected softly. "The one

we're both feeling…and, on my part, having one hell of a time resisting. What do you want to do about it?"

"I don't know," she managed. "I…need to think, and I can't. All I know is that I have no business wanting you to touch me."

"And I have no business wanting to touch you. But I do."

"So, I…we both need time to gather our thoughts."

"Mine are pretty gathered right at the moment."

The silvery edge of anticipation shot up her spine, mixing in her stomach with a frisson of panic. She dragged her gaze from his, looked at the phone on the small table beside the bed while her brain struggled to remember that all actions carried consequences. "If you want, I can call Michael Longstreet's office right now so you can talk to him about his plane."

"What I want right now is to kiss you."

Her heart leapt into her throat while an alarm blared in her head. She didn't want this, didn't want to be seduced by a man with whom there was no future. She dug her nails into her palms. What she wanted didn't seem to matter, not when just his words could breathe life into old needs that had lain dormant inside her for so long.

"I…didn't come here so you could kiss me," she said, even as she leaned into him.

"No, you delivered lunch." He cupped her chin in his hand, kept his eyes open and on hers when he kissed her softly. "What did you bring me, Ireland?"

Her lashes fluttered shut. "Lemon…basil chicken."

"Smells great," he murmured.

The way his mouth worked leisurely down her

throat, she knew darn well he wasn't talking about the chicken.

She let her breath out between her teeth to keep from moaning. "Hope you like it."

"Best I've tasted." His hand came up, sliding beneath her hair to cup the back of her neck. His long fingers were strong and just a little rough, his grip determined. "I want more."

"Help yourself."

His mouth fit perfectly over hers. There was nothing soft about him. His mouth, his hands, his body when he pulled her against him were hard and demanding, his kiss raw and primitive. She wondered if there was a woman alive who would want to be kissed any other way.

Her lips parted hungrily, inviting him in so that she could scrape her teeth over his tongue. He tasted like he looked—dark and dangerous. The tangy scent of him filled her head; visions of their engaging in wild raging sex on the bed just inches away had her senses spinning. Her fingers dug into his waist, holding on as tightly as though she were being tossed around by a storm.

His low groan vibrated through her. His hand tunneled up into her hair, fisted there. He arched her head farther back, then plundered.

She surrendered to him, her mouth opening beneath his as she kissed him with all the need and bafflement that pumped inside her.

She felt urgency ignite within him as his arm locked around her waist. He increased the pressure on her back until their bodies were pressed center to center. Thighs molded against thighs; her nipples tightened against his muscled chest. When she felt his hard arousal against her belly, heat spiraled inside her while her body strained and trembled against his. How could she have forgotten what it was like to be wanted like this?

"Let me have you," he murmured against her mouth. "Ireland, let me have you now."

She wanted to say yes. Wanted him, wanted to steep herself in that dark, dangerous taste. It had been so long since she had felt a man's hands on her flesh, an eternity since she had felt this churning frenzy to mate. Yet, this was more, much more, and through her swirling emotions she felt a desperation that sent ice-pick jabs of panic into her chest.

"No." Her hands trembled when she lifted them to frame his face. She felt dizzy, weak, shaken. "Not yet. I...Rory, I can't."

A few seconds passed before his hand unfisted from her hair. "You're not ready," he said, then rested his brow on hers.

"This has all happened so fast. Too fast." She closed her eyes against the need that churned inside of her. "I can't think. I *have* to think."

"I'm not going to tell you to take your time."

Because she was still wrapped in his arms, she leaned back, pulled slightly away. "It's just...I don't take intimacy lightly."

"I didn't think you did." His eyes burned over her face and settled on her lips. "Trust me, Ireland, you're not a woman a man could take lightly."

She stepped from his touch, forced a smile while her legs wobbled. He had made her want, and want badly.

She needed to be reasonable, she reminded herself. She had to think not only of the present, but the future. He would leave, return to D.C. What would she do about this desperate wanting after he was no longer a part of her life?

Weak with desire, she reached out, braced an unsteady hand on the bed's footboard. Her heart was beating in her head, echoing in her ears. She needed air and space. "I have the mayor's phone number in my office. I'll go downstairs and find it for you."

Rory gave her a long, even look. "Things have moved fast between us. I understand that you might need more time." Reaching out, he wrapped his hand around hers, then dipped his head. When he skimmed his lips over her knuckles, her heart stuck in her throat. "You're trembling," he said quietly.

She closed her eyes, opened them. "I know."

"This isn't over, Ireland. I want you. I'm going to ask you again. Count on it."

"Okay." She slicked her tongue over her swollen lips, and ordered herself to breathe. "I want you to ask."

That evening Rory wanted Peggy with the same intensity he'd felt when he'd held her in his arms, pressed his mouth against hers and found the fit perfect and complete.

He had thought about her all during the long afternoon as he prepared water samples for transportation to the Bureau's lab in San Francisco. Couldn't get her out of his head while he submitted a request to the FBI's database for background checks on the names on

Blake Fallon's lists. As he worked, foremost in Rory's mind was a building need to feel Peggy's soft skin grow hot and moist under his hands. He wanted to trace every subtle curve and dip while her pulse pounded for him. Just for him.

She had tasted like smooth, fine aged whiskey. And left him thirsty for more.

Wasn't much he could do about that thirst at the moment, he thought wryly.

Not while he and the delectable Mrs. Honeywell were two out of about fifty people inching their way along a crowded hallway in the Prosperino Community Center. A few steps in front of them, Samantha and Gracie Warren, holding hands and giggling, nudged their way toward the gymnasium where the winter arts festival had set up the children's activity area.

Rory didn't even attempt to use the jostling crowd as an excuse for the reason he had his hand pressed at the small of Peggy's back. She was incredibly soft, enticingly firm, and he *needed* to touch her. She wore a soft, calf-length dress as green as her eyes; beneath his palm, he felt the elegant sway of her hips as she walked beside him. Dammit, he wanted to do a hell of a lot more than just touch.

The girls darted through an open doorway. The instant Peggy and Rory caught up, Samantha began bouncing on her heels, her dark eyes snapping with excitement. "There's the face-painting lady!"

Standing just behind Samantha, Rory had a perfect view of the pink backpack she wore strapped over her denim jumper. From one side of the backpack, Bugs and Bugsy peered out at him through the bobbing ends of the child's long, dark curls.

Unable to resist, Rory bent down. "So, what color are you girls going to have the lady paint your faces?"

His question brought on another round of giggles. "She doesn't paint your face, Mr. Rory," Samantha said, scrunching her nose at him. "She paints stuff *on* your face."

"I see." He flicked a finger down her downy-soft cheek. "What kind of stuff?"

"Flowers, 'n' stars, 'n'—"

"Birds, too!" Gracie interjected, her blond curls dancing.

Pursing his lips, Rory took in the array of carnival-like booths lining the walls. Here, a child could participate in a variety of undertakings that included casting a line for plastic fish, tossing water balloons at a clown and moon walking. The noise generated by the activities at the booths and the loud talk of the crowd echoed off the gym's high roof.

He turned to Peggy. "Something tells me we'll be tied up here for a while."

"I'm afraid so." She gestured to the small tables clustered in the center of the gym. The red-and-white striped umbrellas and pots of red silk tulips centered on each table lent a sidewalk café atmosphere. Nearby, carts had been set up from which food and drink vendors conducted a brisk business with the adults and children gathered around them.

"Why don't you and I have a cup of coffee while the girls get their faces painted?" Peggy suggested. "I'll tell them to check in with us before they go to any of the other booths. We have a full view of everything in the gym from one of these tables, so we won't have to follow them around.''

"Sounds good to me." When a crease formed between her brows, he hesitated. "Something about that arrangement not working for you?"

"I'm taking it for granted you want to stay here. The galleries along Main Street are all open—that's where the formal art judging takes place. This community center stays opens during the festival so the kids will have a place to go while the adults drop by the galleries. You might prefer to view some serious art instead of watching face-painting and listening to cakewalk music.''

Rory gave her a slow smile while he nudged one side of her dark hair over her shoulder. "After what happened between us at lunch, I'm sticking with you, Ireland.''

Color pooled in her cheeks as her fingers played with the strap of her purse. "Okay." She moistened her lips. "I'll get the girls started at the face-painting booth, then be back to join you.''

"Fine." He slid a hand into the pocket of his slacks. "Why don't you let me treat Samantha and Gracie to the art of their choice?''

"Thanks for offering, but no." Peggy flashed him a grateful smile. "Gracie's mom and I have this covered. We're treating the girls to the artist's double-deluxe-paint-job-for-two special.''

Rory chuckled. "Can't wait to see the results.''

"I guarantee you'll get a good look at them. After

her visit to the booth last year, Samantha didn't wash her face for twenty-four hours.''

Just then, the topic of conversation dashed up, tugged on Peggy's hand. ''Momma, come on!''

''I'll have a latté,'' Peggy said over her shoulder before Samantha dragged her into the crowd.

Rory walked to a cart, waited in line, then placed their orders. Moments later he carried foam cups filled with steaming lattés to an empty table. From where he sat, occasional breaks in the crowd gave him a view of the booth where Peggy engaged in conversation with a smiling woman dressed in a paint-spotted smock. While she spoke, Peggy laid a hand on Samantha's shoulder in a proprietary gesture that had Rory's eyes narrowing.

Had his mother not died when he was an infant, he might have known that kind of love. As it was, his father had been far more comfortable working in the FBI's lab than interacting with a son, so Rory had been shuttled between boarding schools and summer camps. Even latching on to the same career as his father had failed to create more than a tentative link between them.

He glanced back at the booth. Peggy was now crouched between the girls, flipping through pages of what Rory suspected contained examples of the face-painting art. Both girls pointed at a page while nodding vigorously. Laughing, Peggy gave Gracie a hug, then dropped a kiss on her daughter's puckered mouth.

The intimate family ritual had Rory shifting in his chair. His world was so remote from theirs. Alien. Prosperino wasn't his place. He had no place. Didn't want one. Even so, this was the first time in his life he had arrived somewhere and didn't already have his eye on the door, looking toward his next destination.

That sudden realization twisted the muscles in his stomach. Jabbing his fingers though his hair, he told himself the feeling was just another facet of the restless discontent that had gnawed at him for the past couple of months. He sipped his latté, cementing his intention to call his boss and take more time off the job after he finished his business in Prosperino. He was damn well going to figure out what the hell was going on, and get his life back on an even keel that suited him.

"Are you Rory Sinclair?"

Rory looked up, his thoughts scattering. A man, broad-shouldered and well over six feet tall, stood beside the table. He had a sharp-featured face, wide mouth and sun-streaked brown hair that skimmed the collar of his denim shirt.

"Yes."

The man extended a hand. "I'm Michael Longstreet. Prosperino's mayor."

Rory raised a brow. Longstreet's well-worn jeans and boots made him look more like one of the area ranchers than a politician.

"Nice to meet you." Rising, Rory returned the handshake, then gestured to the empty chair across from him. "Have a seat."

"Thanks." Longstreet settled easily into the chair. "Sorry I didn't get back to you when you called my office. My secretary noted in the message you left that you're staying at Honeywell House. When I walked in here a few minutes ago, I saw you talking to Peggy and put two and two together."

"And came up with the right answer." Rory inclined his head toward the vending carts. "Want a cup of coffee?"

"No, thanks. Since this crisis with the water hit, I've been living on the stuff. Cut me, it's a good bet I'll bleed caffeine." The mayor paused to nod to the couple sitting a few tables away, then looked back at Rory. "Let me see if I've got the information you left with my secretary straight. You're a private chemist, hired by Blake Fallon to run tests on the water at Hopechest Ranch."

"That's right."

"You have a current pilot's license, of which you've already faxed a copy to my office. You want to rent my private plane so you can conduct those tests in a San Francisco lab."

"So far, you're batting a thousand."

"Since you're staying at Honeywell House, I figure you've run into Charlie O'Connell by now."

"A couple of times."

"O'Connell has the EPA's lab at his disposal, and he's got an almost two-week head start on you. So far, all he's been able to tell us is what *didn't* cause the contamination. I've got a town in which nothing's going to be right again until someone can tell us what the hell happened to the water on Hopechest Ranch. Do you think you can come up with the answer quicker than the EPA?"

"Probably not." Rory ran a hand over his jaw. "O'Connell has a problem with high-paid consultants who try to steal his thunder. Because of that, he isn't forthcoming with me. I've got a lot of questions he could answer, but won't. That means I have to backtrack over ground he's already covered and come up with those answers for myself. Like you said, O'Connell's been here nearly two weeks longer than me. It's more than likely he'll come back with the answers you need before I do.''

Longstreet nodded. ''Bottom line is I don't care who comes up with the answers, as long as I get them.''

''You shouldn't care,'' Rory agreed. ''As long as the answers you get are the right ones.''

''There is that.'' The mayor leaned back in his chair and stretched out his long legs. ''I've always believed in the value of having a backup plan. Maybe if the EPA's lab misses something, you'll catch it. And vice versa.''

''It could happen.'' Rory leaned in. ''I understand if you've got qualms about renting your plane. Our going for a checkout ride with me in the pilot's seat might take care of that. For a personal reference, talk to Blake Fallon. We go back a long way.''

''I've already spoken to Blake and checked you out with the FAA. You passed.'' Longstreet angled his chin. ''You ever fly a Bonanza?''

Rory smiled. ''I happen to own one.''

''Even better.'' The mayor rose. ''Do you need directions to Prosperino's airport?''

''No, I passed it on the way into town.''

''Meet me there in the morning at seven for that checkout ride. If you pass, you've got access to the Bonanza for as long as you need it.''

"Great. How much?"

"Just find out what happened to the water on Hope-chest Ranch. That's all I care about," Longstreet added before striding off.

Rory pursed his mouth. Instinct told him the citizens of Prosperino had voted themselves in one hell of a mayor.

"This place is a madhouse," Peggy said over the din as she slid into the chair beside him.

"Your town has its fair share of kids," Rory commented.

"And if you're not used to it, all this activity can be overwhelming." She sipped her latté, her mouth settling into a satisfied curve. "Are you sure you wouldn't rather take off on your own and go through the galleries? We have some wonderful artists in town. You might find a painting or a piece of sculpture that would look perfect in your home."

"I don't have a home."

Her smile faded. "Everyone has a home."

"I lease a furnished apartment in Virginia. If I had to, I could box up everything I own in a couple of hours, load it onto my plane and never think twice about leaving that apartment. I don't think that's most people's definition of a home."

"No, it's not." Her green eyes examined his face over the rim of her cup. "What about your family? Do you consider where they are home?"

"Family is another thing I don't have."

"No one?"

"My parents are dead. I was an only child."

"Surely you've got some cousins somewhere. Maybe an aunt or uncle?"

"An aunt and one cousin. I lost track of them years ago."

"That's too bad."

Rory angled his chin. "My not having a family sounds dire to you because your business centers around making a temporary home for strangers. The truth is, there are people in this world who don't have, or even care about having, what you define as a home. I'm one of them." He lifted a shoulder. "I've never wanted the responsibility or restrictions of one."

"What restrictions?"

He found the look in her eyes too serious for his liking. "You're tied to one place. You can't just walk away, come and go as you please. Sounds restrictive to me."

"I just think it's sad not to have a place where you can dig in and know you belong."

"I do have one. It's called a laboratory. They're all over the world."

Because the subject had wedged an unexpected ball of discomfort in his stomach, Rory shifted his gaze to the milling crowd. He caught sight of Kade Lummus, standing at the dart-throwing booth decorated with colorful balloons. Even out of his creased-to-perfection uniform, the guy looked fit beyond reason. A little boy who Rory estimated to be about Samantha's age stood beside Lummus, gripping one leg of his jeans.

Rory swept a hand in their direction. "Is that Lummus's son?"

Peggy hesitated a heartbeat before shifting her gaze. "No, his nephew. Kade doesn't have any children."

"He married?"

"No."

Rory remet her gaze. "He's interested in you. I figure you know that."

"Yes."

"Is the feeling mutual?"

"Kade and I are just friends."

Rory remembered the controlled anger he had seen in Lummus's eyes last night while Peggy recounted the details of her assault. The cop's feelings for her went a hell of a lot deeper than friendship.

"You're friends for now," Rory amended.

"Now and forever."

"So, I guess the guy's just not your type?"

"He's a cop."

Rory raised an eyebrow. "And?"

"And nothing. Kade wears a badge."

"You have something against cops?"

"They die." She closed her eyes, opened them, then set her cup aside. "That sounds awful, but it's true. My husband was a police officer."

"I take it he died in the line of duty," Rory said quietly.

"Yes." She eased out a breath. "Nearly five years ago. Jay was a sergeant on the LAPD. He was killed less than one week after I found out I was pregnant with Samantha. He never even got a chance to see his child. And she missed out on having a father."

Rory felt his chest tighten while he watched the play of emotion in Peggy's face. "I'm sorry."

"So am I."

He glanced up in time to see Lummus laugh, then swing his nephew onto his broad shoulders before heading out of the door of the gym.

"Some things I'll never forget. I won't let myself forget."

Rory looked back at Peggy. She was staring into her coffee now, a wrenching sadness in her green eyes. She had spoken the words so softly, he'd barely missed them.

"What things?"

"Opening the door at three o'clock in the morning to find the police chaplain and a deputy chief standing on my porch." The hand she'd rested on the table inches from Rory's tightened into a fist. "Going through twenty hours of labor without being able to hold the hand of the father of my child. Then, years later, having to explain to that child why her daddy went away." Her brow furrowed. "No cops. Never again."

Rory rubbed a hand over his face. It had to be the height of irony, he decided. Peggy had no idea *he* was a cop. He'd had no clue the woman he'd almost ravished only hours ago—and had obsessed over since—was a cop's widow. A widow who had sworn to never again get involved with a man who carried a badge.

Great.

The thought of the kisses they'd shared had him clamping down on a hard tug of guilt. Because he'd kept the truth from her, she hadn't known—couldn't have known—that by moving into his arms she had stepped into territory she'd forbidden to herself. Then he hadn't known, either.

Now he did.

So, what was he going to do about it?

He set his jaw. It wasn't in his nature to take advantage of a woman. With those he had involved himself with in the past, that had never been an issue since he'd gone out of his way to choose women with philosophies similar to his own. One didn't have to factor emotional entanglements into the formula if the parties involved moved freely through life with no regrets, no baggage.

Rory now knew that the woman sitting in silence beside him had plenty of baggage.

He had no doubt that, had Peggy known he was an FBI special agent, she never would have let him get close enough to exchange the searing kisses they'd shared. And she sure as hell wouldn't have encouraged him to ask her again to go to bed with him. Which was a question he had fully intended to ask again. Soon. Maybe even after they got back to the inn that night.

Not anymore, he decided grimly.

He had given his word to Blake Fallon, and he would keep it. That meant staying in Prosperino for as long as it took to find out what had contaminated the water on Hopechest Ranch. Since the question of whether Charlie O'Connell was on the up-and-up remained unanswered, Rory knew he needed to stay at Honeywell House until he found out that answer.

He slid Peggy a sideways look. She had shifted her attention to the face-painting booth; now her mouth curved into a smile as she watched her daughter.

Against his thighs, Rory's hands fisted. He could still taste that lush mouth, still feel the texture of her skin beneath his palms.

His tough luck, he told himself. He would have to be content with those memories, because it was all of her he would ever get.

As of this minute, the gorgeous, sexy-as-hell widow Honeywell was off-limits.

Seven

Three days, Peggy thought as she shifted linens and towels into the crook of one arm while using her pass-key to open the door of Rory's room. Three days had passed since he'd held her. Kissed her. Three long days and eternally longer nights during which she had spent most of her time wondering what had caused Rory to put up the wall between them.

It wasn't her imagination, she was sure of that. She had felt the invisible barrier the instant it had gone up while she sat beside him in the gym amid the chaos of the arts festival activities. After that, Rory had kept the conversation between them light and genial. Friendly. There had been nothing in his voice to suggest he'd had second thoughts about his kissing her until her eyes rolled back in her head earlier that day. Nothing in his steady gaze that hinted he had changed his mind about wanting her. Yet, in one hammer beat of her heart, her senses focused, and she knew he had taken an emotional step back.

More like a giant leap.

Pulling in a deep breath, Peggy swung open the door and stepped into his room. As always, she found he'd left things relatively neat. The only things sharing space with the sprawling ivy plant on the desk opposite the bed were his small computer and printer. He never left her guest towels wadded on the bathroom floor. Never left wet rings on the tabletops. The perfect guest.

Try as she might, she couldn't stop her gaze from settling on the open bathroom door. No matter that she knew he wasn't there, no matter that she willed herself not to, she pictured Rory standing in the doorway, a towel hitched low on his hips, his broad chest tanned and darkened by sleek black hair. And his mouth—that hard, firm mouth—lifted into an unrepentant grin.

The memory sent a pang of desire through her that had her fingers digging into the linens she carried.

Why, oh why, had he put up the wall?

The question set her jaw. Dammit, she needed to get a grip. She had asked herself that one question a hundred times and still had no answer. Since Mr. Sinclair was making himself scarce these days, she didn't figure on getting any information from *him*.

She had caught only glimpses of him since the night of the arts festival. Instead of coming down to breakfast the past three mornings, he had left the inn at dawn, presumably heading for the airport where he picked up Mayor Longstreet's airplane for the flight to San Francisco. When Rory returned at night, it was always well past the time she served wine and cheese in the study. He used the front door and went straight up to his room. And he had avoided setting foot in the kitchen for a helping of the apricot cobbler she had baked. For him.

Her mood darkened to match the late-afternoon gloom that pressed against the windows of the third-floor room. With nerve-aching frustration pounding in her head, she dumped the linens and towels in the tufted slipper chair that sat in one corner, then stepped to the bed. There, she shoved the star-patterned quilt aside and jerked off the top and bottom sky-blue sheets.

She was tired of brooding over Rory Sinclair. Sick of wondering if he had built the deliberate distance between them because he'd taken exception to her re-action to his having no home, no family. Ridiculous, she told herself.

After all, why would the man care what her view was on that subject? It wasn't as if she had tried to force her opinion on him. If he wanted to spend his life living in an impersonal furnished apartment and calling some sterile laboratory home, more power to him.

No, she reasoned, as she grabbed the first of the pair of pillows and jerked off the blue-and-white striped case. Rory hadn't put the skids on the relationship that had begun developing between them because she pre-ferred being rooted to one place and he didn't. The only other thing they had discussed while sitting at the table in the gym was Jay and the reason she had no intention of ever getting involved with another cop. Since she could see no reason that topic could matter either way to a chemist, all she could think was that Rory had simply changed his mind.

He didn't want her.

So, fine, she told herself as she snagged up the second pillow while trying to ignore the little slashing knives of hurt that snuck through her guard. He didn't want her. His obvious disinterest in her uncomplicated things to no end.

The scent of Rory's subtle, woodsy cologne wafted up from the pillowcase and slid into her lungs. Her hands went still as desire poured through her like heated wine.

The raw need she had felt when he held her in his arms and his mouth devoured hers came back a hundredfold. That need was deeper and more complex than anything she'd ever known. Clutching the pillow, she reached for the bed's brass footboard, then closed her eyes. Caught between common sense and feelings, she needed a moment until reason overcame her own choking desire.

Rory had said he wanted her. He had acted like he did. Yet, for whatever reason, he had decided the hot, searing kisses they had shared on almost the exact spot she now stood were the beginning and the end of any personal involvement between them. She needed to accept that, *had* to accept it. Why he had changed his mind didn't matter. What mattered was that he had changed it.

She knew that once her hormones settled down and she started thinking logically again, she would be grateful he had taken that step back. She had a business to run and a daughter to raise. The last thing she needed was to spend time pining for a man who lived a continent away. A man over whom she seemed to have totally lost her head.

But not her heart, she countered instantly. That knowledge sent a wave of relief rolling through her. She hadn't lost her heart to Rory. Thank God things hadn't gotten that far.

She took long, cleansing breaths as she made quick work of putting crisp floral sheets on the bed. Just as she leaned to smooth the edges of the quilt, the sound of hurried footsteps coming down the hallway sent her heart into her throat. Rory.

Peggy jerked around, then went utterly still when Charlie O'Connell's tall form blocked the doorway.

For a moment, the shapes and colors in the room seemed to shift out of sync as fear caught her by the throat. She took a step back, halting when the bed's footboard caught her in the spine. She curled her fingers, then flexed them while telling herself to calm down. The EPA inspector had done nothing to frighten her—she was just still skittish from the attack in the greenhouse.

"A problem's come up." While he spoke, he shoved back the cuff of his green sweater to check his watch. "I need you to help me out."

"I will if I can, Mr. O'Connell."

"I've got an appointment in fifteen minutes. It's important and I can't be late." He glanced again at his watch. "I went down, tried to start my car. Nothing."

"There's a mechanic in town. I can call him for you. He'll come out to look at your car."

"Fine, do that. But I don't have time right now to

figure out what's wrong." He shoved a hand through his dark hair. "I need to borrow your station wagon for an hour. Two at the most."

"My car?"

"I'll pay you." He jammed a hand in the pocket of his slacks, pulled out some bills. "Same rate as I'm paying for that worthless piece of metal parked out in the lot."

"I don't want your money."

"Dammit, woman, I don't have time to arrange for another car," he snapped, impatience flashing in his eyes. "This meeting is important. It's possible I'll get some answers about the water problems at Hopechest Ranch."

Peggy bit back the tart reply on the tip of her tongue. If loaning her station wagon would help O'Connell get the answers the whole town had been waiting for, it was the least she could do.

"Let's go down to my office. I keep an extra set of keys there."

Three hours after Peggy handed her keys to Charlie O'Connell, Rory steered his own car into the dim, gravel-packed parking lot in front of a dubious-looking brick building. Long fingers of shadow spread across the lot, illuminated only by two neon beer signs in the blackened windows and a bare bulb over the front door.

Raising a brow, Rory climbed out the car into the cool evening air that hinted of rain. Minutes after he had touched down in the mayor's plane, Blake Fallon had called him on his cell phone and invited him to meet for drinks and dinner at a tavern named Jake's.

"The pride of Prosperino," Blake added after he rat-
tled off directions.

Despite the appearance of the place, Rory was glad
Blake had called. It meant putting off returning to
Honeywell House for a few more hours. Three days,
he thought as he slid his car keys into a pocket of his
leather jacket. Three days since Peggy told him she had
buried one cop and would never again involve herself
with another. Three nights during which he had paced
his room, thinking of her, imagining her lying in a bed
a few floors below. He carried the taste of her inside
him. The need to put his hands on her was killing him,
inch by slow inch.

He couldn't touch her. Wouldn't. Even if he had
planned to stay in Prosperino for good—which he
didn't—nothing changed the fact he was a cop. He
might work out of a lab, but he carried a badge and a
gun, just as her husband had.

The badge gave Rory connections. Without qualm,
he had called a contact at the LAPD and obtained a
faxed copy of the incident report detailing Jay Honeywell's death. Honeywell had been a sergeant, working
undercover narcotics. A fellow cop read a situation
wrong, jumped to unsupported conclusions, which led
to the bust of what was thought to be a cocaine operation in a warehouse. Instead of the expected distri-
bution center, what the cops found when they raided
the place were street druggies cooking crank. One suspect fired a shot that ignited open containers of ether.
The resulting explosion killed Sergeant Honeywell, two
fellow officers and one bad guy.

Setting his jaw, Rory headed for the tavern's dimly

lit door, the loose gravel crunching beneath his feet. He knew he could have her. The knowledge was based not on conceit, but the memory of how Peggy had trembled in his arms when he'd held her. If he closed his eyes, he could feel her body shuddering against his while her nipples tightened and her lips opened beneath his.

Yes, he knew he could have her. Knew, too, that even if they became lovers, chances were good he would leave Prosperino with her having no clue he carried a badge.

Problem was *he* knew. If he took her to bed knowing how she felt about cops, he would never be able to face himself again in a mirror.

He should get the hell away from Honeywell House. Check out tonight, then bunk with Blake at Hopechest Ranch. The downside to that scenario was it would limit his observation of Charlie O'Connell.

Rory rubbed at the knots in the back of his neck. Who was he trying to kid? He had no evidence to suggest O'Connell was anything other than a disgruntled civil servant who refused to share information. Rory knew damn well that Peggy and Samantha were the reason he hadn't left Honeywell House. The lady art judges had checked out the day after the arts festival. The honeymooning couple, the day after that. No new guests had arrived since then. Other than himself, Charlie O'Connell was the only guest. The idea of the bastard trying to hustle Peggy while he groped at her had Rory muttering a derisive curse.

Stepping beneath the bare bulb, he pulled open the heavy wooden door. He was instantly greeted by the slam and crack of pool balls and air redolent with a lifetime of tobacco.

Pausing, he waited just inside the door while his eyes adjusted to the dim interior. On his right was a long, scarred bar where several men huddled on stools, talking over their beers; on his left sat two pool tables with glaring fluorescent lights hanging overhead. Both tables were in use.

Rory shifted his gaze, caught sight of Blake Fallon and another man sitting at a table in the back of the bar.

Rory strode past several tables, all occupied. The customers' dress ran the gamut from work shirts and jeans to tailored suits. A real cultural mix, he thought. He stopped by the bar, ordered a beer, then carried his glass to Blake's table.

Blake nodded toward the man sitting across from him. "Rory Sinclair, meet Rafe James."

Still standing, Rory extended his hand. "Good to meet you."

"Same here."

The copper skin, midnight black hair and high slash of cheekbones evidenced Rafe James's Native American heritage. The cool mahogany eyes that gazed out of the sharp-angled face gave the impression they could carve a man into pieces at ten paces.

Rory settled his jacket over the back of an empty chair, then took a seat. "I have to tell you, Fallon, if this dive is the pride of Prosperino, I'm packing my bags and leaving tonight."

Despite the fatigue that shadowed his eyes, Blake grinned. "You weren't paying attention on the phone,

Sinclair. I said Jake's *sirloin burgers* are the pride of Prosperino. Rafe and I already ordered ours. I told the waitress to bring you one, too.''

"I'll reserve my thanks until I taste the thing.'' Rory took a peanut from the plastic bowl on the table, cracked it.

Mentally, he scanned the list of names Blake had given him of people who could profit if he lost his job. Then the names of those who might take revenge on Blake for the two attempts his father had made on Joe Colton's life. Rafe James hadn't made either list.

Rory scooped up another peanut. "So, Rafe, what's your connection with my college buddy here?''

"We raised hell together growing up.'' Rafe slid Blake a look. "Now I raise Appaloosas on my own ranch. I get into a lot less trouble these days.''

"True,'' Blake agreed. "But you don't have near as much fun.''

"You have a point.''

Blake's smile faded as he met Rory's gaze. "People come from all over the country to buy Rafe's Appaloosas. He's holding his breath, just like everybody else, that the water on his ranch keeps testing okay.''

"I wish I could tell you what caused the contamination at Hopechest,'' Rory said, then tipped back his beer. "I can't. Yet. Right now all I can do is give you a list of things that didn't cause it.'' He paused, furrowing his brow. "It's great that every other water source in the area has tested fine, but that concerns me, too.''

"You're thinking the contamination was done on purpose,'' Blake said. "That someone targeted Hopechest Ranch. Or me. If that's the case, I need to shut down the entire operation. Get the kids and staff out of there before, God forbid, something worse happens.''

''Don't jump the gun until we know something for sure.'' Rory shifted in his chair. ''I'm a chemist, Blake. All I can do is identify the contaminant. That's the first step. The second one is figuring out how the stuff got into the water. If it turns out whatever the hell it is spread there from an underground source, you'll probably need a geologist or a hydrologist—or both—to explain how aquifers and water tables work.'' Rory frowned. ''And I'll want a question or two answered myself.''

''For instance?'' Blake asked.

''Right now, a new well is being drilled on the Crooked Arrow Reservation. The well site is just yards from Hopechest property. The water at that drill site tests okay. If it turns out the contaminant came from a nearby underground source, someone's going to have to explain to me how and why it got into one well, but not the other.''

Rafe looked at Blake. ''That's the well Springer's paying to have drilled.''

''Springer,'' Rory repeated. ''I saw that name on the side of a pickup truck when I took water samples at the well site. What's Springer?''

''An oil company,'' Blake answered. ''Operates a refining plant outside of town.''

Rory raised a brow. ''So, why is an oil company drilling a water well on an Indian reservation?''

''In a name, David Corbett.'' Rafe inclined his head

toward the front of the bar. "That's him shooting pool at the far table. The guy wearing the starched white shirt with its sleeves rolled up."

Rory caught a glimpse of an athletically built man, just above six feet tall. His loosened navy tie and the conservative cut auburn hair pegged him as an executive.

"He a good guy?" Rory asked.

Rafe nodded. "I do security work as a sideline and I've worked off and on at Springer. I filled in there for a couple of weeks when one of their guards got sick and they were in a bind. Springer had just decided to expand its operations, and it made an offer to lease some land that belongs to the Crooked Arrow Reservation. Corbett's a high-up VP at Springer, so I guess that's why he personally delivered the offer to the elders at the res. The elders said no."

Rory angled his chin. "By the way you sound, I take it Corbett didn't go away mad?"

"No. In fact, he was so appalled by the living conditions of some of the Native Americans that he came back with an offer from Springer to drill a new water well on res land. Free of charge. That's the well you saw being drilled."

"Corbett's a righteous guy," Blake agreed. His eyes narrowed. "I sure can't say much for his choice of pool partners, though."

Rory looked again toward the front of the bar. His gaze settled on the wiry-framed man with light brown hair who was leaning over the pool table. He executed his break, then gave Corbett a smug smile that accompanied the clatter of balls.

Rory tapped an index finger against his glass. "Holly," he said to Blake. "Your secretary's name is Holly, right?"

"That's right."

"She has the same eyes and jawline of the man playing pool with David Corbett."

"Showoff," Blake muttered. "Yeah, that's Holly's father. His name's Todd Lamb."

Rory watched Lamb circle the pool table, calculating his next shot while he chalked his cue. Neither David Corbett nor Todd Lamb had made either of Blake's lists.

Rory looked back at Blake. "You have something against Lamb?"

"Nothing personal." Blake raised a shoulder. "I just don't like the way he ignores his daughter. Holly deserves better."

Rory kept his expression neutral as he scooped another peanut out of the bowl. He remembered the way Holly's gaze had lingered on Blake, the softening in her voice when she spoke to him. Rory suspected the potential was there for more than just a boss-employee relationship.

"Here's your order, boys." A redhead with expressive, flirty eyes and a black leather skirt that barely made it past the legal limit sauntered up to the table, a loaded tray in her hands. "Three of Jake's special sirloin burgers. And fries." When she leaned and settled the plates on the table, her skinny black top dipped down low over firm, well-developed breasts.

Rory pursed his mouth when she ambled away on

skyscraper heels. "Are you *boys* sure it's these sirloin burgers that are the pride of Prosperino?"

Rafe chuckled. "Scout's honor."

Rory took a bite and found himself pleasantly surprised. "This is great. I'm starved."

Blake looked at Rafe. "Can you believe you heard that statement from someone staying at Honeywell House?"

"No." Rafe washed down a bite with a swallow of beer. "The last time I was there, Peggy served me a piece of key lime pie. Best I've ever tasted. I made such a big deal over it, she sent the rest of the pie home with me."

"That's Peggy," Blake agreed. "Nobody leaves Honeywell House hungry." He shot Rory a look. "You sample her apricot cobbler yet?"

"Haven't had a chance."

"When you were in my office, you said you and Peggy struck a deal. You test the inn's water twice a day, she bakes you the dessert of your choice every night."

"That's the deal."

"So, what happened?"

"I test the inn's water twice a day. It's fine, in case you were wondering."

"What about dessert?"

Rory thought of the past nights he'd paced his room, thinking about Peggy. Wanting her. He knew that after he left Prosperino, he would lie awake a lot of nights, thinking about being with her.

"I decided it'd be best if I passed on dessert," he said quietly. "All it takes is willpower. A lot of willpower."

Eight

"Mr. O'Connell said he needed to borrow my station wagon for an hour. Two at the most." Standing at the center island, Peggy turned and checked the clock on the oven, saw it was nearly nine o'clock. She looked back across the kitchen at the table where Kade Lummus sat. "It's been over five hours."

Looking relaxed and comfortable in his worn jeans and gray sweater, Kade took the last bite of the warm bread pudding with white chocolate sauce she had served him when he arrived. "You're sure O'Connell didn't mention anything about who he planned to meet?" Kade asked, nudging his bowl aside. "Or where?"

"No. I didn't ask. Looking back, I should have, since he wanted to borrow my car to get there." She shoved her hair behind her shoulders. "After he said he might finally find out some answers about what happened to the water on Hopechest Ranch, all I wanted was for him to get to his meeting.''

"I would have felt the same way. Everyone's holding their breath over the water contamination. Waiting for answers is like sitting on a fault line, wondering when the next earthquake will hit.''

"That sums it up.'' Her concern about the inn's water had eased slightly now that Rory was running tests twice a day and slipping the results on notes under her office door. Still, she was like everyone else—worried about the safety of the town's water supply. If the contaminant suddenly spread, the entire population of Prosperino might have to evacuate. A knot formed in her throat at the possibility. The inn was more than just a means of support for her and Samantha. They had built a life in her grandmother's house that nestled on the cliff overlooking the Pacific Ocean. Peggy couldn't imagine leaving and not knowing when she could return.

She picked up a pot holder, slid it into a drawer near the cooktop. "Kade, I feel bad about calling you at home. I wanted your advice on what to do about Mr. O'Connell's being gone so long. I didn't intend for you to drive over here.''

As she spoke, rain started to patter on the roof, sounding like fingers lightly drumming on a table. Peggy walked to the window over the sink, nudged back one side of the striped curtain and glanced out. O'Connell's rental car hunched in the rain beside Kade's police cruiser, the only cars parked in the lot.

She forced away thoughts about Rory, wondering where he was, when he would get back.

Turning, she rubbed at the ache that had settled in her forehead and met Kade's gaze. "Thanks to me, you're going to get wet."

"No big deal." He sipped the coffee she had brewed when he arrived, his dark eyes watching her over the rim of the mug. "Your bread pudding is worth getting a little wet."

She relaxed enough to smile. "Thanks. Would you like more?"

"Yes, but I'll pass. As it is, I have to spend double time at the gym working off this one helping." He flipped the cover closed on the small pad on which he'd jotted notes. "I've got all the information I need on your station wagon. I'll have dispatch put it out on the air tonight."

"I don't want Mr. O'Connell to get into trouble. I *did* loan him the car."

"At this point, the only thing he's guilty of is breaking his word to you. I'll make sure dispatch broadcasts the information as a 'check the welfare of the driver' stop." Kade rose, walked to the back door and snagged his jacket off the nearby coatrack. "My shift starts at seven in the morning. Give me a call. If O'Connell hasn't surfaced, I'll upgrade him to a missing person and put a statewide APB out on your station wagon." As he spoke, Kade pulled on his jacket. "Give Samantha a kiss for me. Tell her I'm sorry I didn't make it here before her bedtime."

"I will. She'll be upset she missed seeing you."

Peggy walked to where he stood, put a hand on his arm. "I appreciate all you do for us, Kade."

He looked down, his steady brown eyes locked with hers. "I don't want your appreciation, Peggy. You know that."

"I know." She dropped her hand, curled it against her thigh. "And you know I can't ever get involved again with a cop. I can't do it, Kade."

He cupped a hand to her cheek, his mouth tightening. "I've thought about giving up the job so you and I would have a chance to see what could happen between us. I can't bring myself to do that. No matter how much I care about you, I can't turn my back on the job. I'm a cop. That's all I'll ever be. It's who I am."

Jay had been the same way, born to wear a badge. He had thrived on the edge of danger that was a natural part of the job. The job that had killed him. His senseless death had left her with a scar on her heart and a hole in her life that would always be there.

"It's no good, Kade," she said softly. "If you walked away from being a cop, you would someday hate me for that."

"Yeah." He dropped his hand, eased out a breath, then changed the subject. "After your attack, we put extra patrols on the inn. None of the guys have spotted anything. We also haven't had any additional sightings of the drifter I told you about. Looks like he's left the area."

"That's a relief."

Kade hesitated. "Before I left the other night, I asked Sinclair to keep his eyes open for anything around here that didn't look right. He's called twice to let me know he hasn't seen anything. He's also grilled me on what we're doing about finding the guy that hurt you.''

Peggy slid her hands into the pockets of her slacks, pulled them back out. She'd had no idea Rory had called Kade. Then again, how could she know, since he'd made himself so scarce the past three days?

''It's nice that so many people are looking out for Samantha and me,'' she said.

''You know you can call me if you need anything. Anytime.'' Without waiting for her to comment, Kade turned, pulled open the door, then shut it tight behind him.

Weary, she rested her forehead against the door. Kade was a good man. An honorable one. She had no doubt that, for as long as he lived, he would be there for her and Samantha. She closed her eyes. Jay had told her he would be there for her always. Yet, he hadn't even lived long enough to see their daughter.

''No cops,'' Peggy said quietly. ''Never again.''

It wasn't lost on her that she had been perfectly able to control the depth of her feelings for Kade, but not for Rory. Why couldn't she make herself stop yearning for a man who would only be a part of her life for so short a time?

''Crazy,'' she murmured. She was an intelligent woman, responsible and, for the most part, logical. Here she was, stupidly, irrationally drawn to a man who could offer her nothing but heartbreak. She'd had enough of that in her life, and she didn't need to go around, leaving herself open for more. Especially from a man who didn't even want her.

Stifling the moan that rose in her throat, Peggy pushed away from the door. Her bruised hip felt stiff, and the headache now brewing dead center in her forehead told her all the sleep she'd lost over the past nights had finally caught up with her.

She moved to the table, carried the dishes Kade had used to the sink, rinsed them and placed them in the dishwasher. That done, she headed toward the front of the inn for her ritual of settling the inn for the night.

Leaving a dim light burning in the foyer, she moved into the study. The fire she'd built earlier simmered in the grate, its warmth drawing her across the room. Rain pattered softly against the windows. Feeling the fatigue in her legs and back, she settled onto the leather couch that faced the fire. She would sit here for a minute or two, she told herself. Sit here, and wait for Charlie O'Connell to return with her station wagon.

Closing her eyes, she leaned her head against the soft leather while deep in her restless heart, the truth stirred. Rory was whom she waited on. Rory whom she wanted to walk through the door. Rory whom she wanted to come home.

The sky broke the same instant Rory walked out of Jake's. He dashed across the tavern's gravel parking lot, slid into his car and shook the rain from his hair. Seconds later, he pulled out of the lot and turned the car onto the dark coastal highway for the short trip to Honeywell House.

He had hoped the stop at Jake's would help his

thoughts steady. Instead, they had constantly turned to Peggy. The memory of her warm, subtle taste, the soft feel of her skin had left his mind as restless as the sea that churned against the ragged cliffs edging the dark shoreline.

His hands tightened on the steering wheel. Here he was, a man who had never wanted the restriction or the responsibility of a home, drawn to a woman who thrived on those very things. Things he had never had. And didn't want, he reminded himself.

He steered around a curve, then headed across a bridge. Below, the angry surf rolled in, crested, then broke. His jaw tightened as his car's headlights stabbed through the darkness and the rain to illuminate the thin ribbon of road leading up to Honeywell House. Something was happening inside of him and he had no idea what it was. All he knew was that no one had ever had a hold on him like this before. No person...or thing, he amended when he pulled into the parking lot and turned off the engine.

The inn sat nestled against the hill, the small spotlights spreading dramatic fans of illumination up three stories to the widow's walk. A light, weak but welcoming, glowed with golden warmth behind the window in the foyer.

It wasn't just the woman who had left that light burning that drew him. It was the home she had made.

"Christ." Rubbing his eyes, he sat in silence while the rain drummed against the car's roof and slid down the windows. For the first time in his life, he knew what it felt like to come home.

He took a mental step back, stunned by the realization, stunned it had been there to come out. He didn't know what was causing the change inside of him. Had no clue how to stop it. Didn't know if he could. Or even if he wanted to. He couldn't deny that he cared about Peggy more than he had ever cared about any other woman. Still, his feelings didn't alter the fact he had lived his entire life on the road to somewhere else. It was a lifestyle that fit him like a glove. That he was now wondering if he could settle in one place, be on the inside looking out was foreign territory and needed to be approached with caution.

As did Peggy's determination to never again involve herself with a man who wore a badge.

In truth, he had no idea what to do about either issue—if, in fact, he should *do* anything. Since it was apparent he wasn't coming up with any solutions sitting in his car, he shouldered open the door and ducked into the rain. Perhaps because his mind had been so weighted down with thought, he didn't notice until this moment that Charlie O'Connell's rental car was the only other vehicle in the lot.

Where the hell was Peggy? he wondered as he dashed up the porch steps. It was nearly ten o'clock— what was she doing out so late with Samantha?

Using his key, Rory swung open the front door and stepped into the foyer where the dim light glowed. He locked the door behind him, his gaze flicking in the direction of her small office. The door was closed, no sliver of light showed beneath.

He took two steps toward the staircase, pausing when he came even with the arched entrance to the study. The waning flames in the fireplace put out just enough light for him to see Peggy curled on the couch.

Because he couldn't help himself, he moved across the study to stand near her.

It was a fitful sleep, he decided as he pulled off his leather jacket and laid it on one of the nearby wing chairs. She was lying on her side, one hand fisted against a small throw pillow. In the flickering light, her skin looked stunningly pale, the shadows deep where her dark lashes fanned across her cheeks. She murmured something indistinguishable; a crease of worry formed between her brows.

A bad dream, he thought as he moved over and crouched in front of her. The need tethered tight inside him strained hard at her scent. She smelled like the inn, of that welcoming combination of lemon, cinnamon and lavender that had greeted him the first night. And was so much a part of what had drawn him back over the past days.

When her head jerked, her dark hair pooled across the pillow like rich mink.

Wanting to soothe her, he traced a fingertip down the deepening crease between her brows.

"No!" Her fist swung out, caught him on one shoulder. "Don't—"

"Wake up, Ireland. You're having a bad dream."

"No! Don't touch me." She shot awake, her eyes wide, glazed and unfocused. At the same instant, she lunged to her feet, rocked a bit.

He gripped her upper arms to steady her. "It's Rory," he said quietly. Her skin had gone deathly pale. "You had a bad dream."

She gulped in a breath, blinked her eyes. "Rory?"

"You had a bad dream," he repeated. His hands slid up, cupping her shoulders. "You're okay now."

"Oh, God. I dreamed..." She shuddered. "He came back."

"Who?"

"The man in the greenhouse. He came back."

When she leaned in and pressed her face into his shoulder, Rory felt the thunder of her heart. He closed his eyes. It felt right having her in his arms. So right. Even as he told himself to step back, he buried his face in the soft fall of her hair. "You're okay. It was just a dream."

"Yes." Her arms slid around his waist. "A bad one."

"Do you want a glass of wine?" He rubbed a hand gently up and down her spine. "Maybe something stronger to steady you?"

She inched her head back to look up at him. The firelight shaded her green eyes with gold. Rising on tiptoe, she pressed a kiss to his throat. "You. I want you."

"Ireland." The feel of her teeth scraping against his throat shot desire through him like a bullet. Knowing he needed to distance himself from an edge that had suddenly spun closer, he forced himself to think about the badge in his pocket. "I'm not the right man for you."

"I know." Her mouth was urgent and frantic and hot against his neck, his jaw. He felt the tremors that coursed down her body, heard her shuddering breaths.

"You'll leave Prosperino. You won't come back. It doesn't matter."

"Eventually it will." Fighting to hold on to control, he gathered her hair in his hand and drew her head back until their eyes met. The desire he saw there made his knees weak. "There's no future for us. I can't promise you any kind of future."

She reached up, framed his face with her hands while her body molded itself to the lines of his. "When Jay died, I made a future for myself and Samantha. I don't need a man to do that for me. I'm not thinking of tomorrow, Rory," she said, her voice low and thick. "I'm thinking of right now. You're who I want right now."

He could have taken her in one greedy gulp. For a brief, blinding instant, he considered falling into the mindless pleasure of her touch and taking what his body ached to have. It was his heart and his mind that held him back.

"This can't happen." He tightened his hands on her arms, gave her a gentle shake. "Not like this."

"I…" She stilled against him while a dull flush crept into her cheeks. Her arms slid from around his waist. She took a step back. Then another. "I'm sorry. You made it clear over the past three days that you don't want…" She dropped her face into her hands. "Oh, God, I can't believe I just attacked you."

"If you think I minded, you're wrong." He shackled his fingers around her wrists, forced her hands down. "Look at me. Ireland, look at me," he repeated, then waited for her gaze to meet his. When it did, the mortification in her eyes made his chest tighten. "Dammit, there's no reason for you to be embarrassed."

"I think there is."

"Maybe this will change your mind." He stepped closer; he couldn't help it. "You're driving me crazy. All I've done for the past three days is think about you. I can barely do my job. Dammit, I can't even *breathe* without wanting you. I've stayed away because I'm not sure I can keep my hands off of you."

Her lips parted as a glimmer of relief spread over her face. "Really?"

"Really."

"I thought…you weren't interested." She closed her eyes, opened them. "This coming from the woman who just tried to jump your bones."

His mouth curved. He freed one of her wrists, used his fingers to nudge a wave of dark hair from her cheek. "I'm not complaining."

"No, you're not. You're just saying no."

"I have reasons."

Shifting his gaze to the row of rain-streaked windows that looked out onto the front porch, he fought the urge to tell her he was an FBI special agent. The instant she knew he carried a badge, she would turn away. He was sure of that. What he wasn't sure of was Charlie O'Connell. Rory had no proof that the EPA inspector had his own agenda in regard to the contaminated water on Hopechest Ranch. Still, Rory couldn't shake the feeling in his gut that told him there was more going on with O'Connell than met the eye.

For all Rory knew, O'Connell could have been the man who attacked Peggy in the greenhouse. O'Connell claimed he had been at the reservation checking the site where Springer was drilling the new water well. Rory had checked, and couldn't find anyone who could verify the EPA inspector's alibi. That didn't mean the man was guilty, but it sure as hell didn't put him in the clear, either.

Rory bit back a frustrated curse. He knew if he told Peggy he was FBI, her behavior toward him would change. It was possible O'Connell would sense that change, and wonder about it. He might start thinking that Peggy was hiding a secret or two about the chemist Blake Fallon had hired. Depending on what O'Connell was up to, any suspicions on his part could put Peggy at risk.

The prospect tightened Rory's throat. For now, it was safer for everyone to continue to think he worked for a private company.

Brow furrowed, he caught Peggy's waiting gaze. "There are things about me that I can't tell you. In the long run, they probably don't matter much since I'm leaving Prosperino as soon as my job here is done."

"I keep reminding myself of that." She was gazing up at him as if she were looking beyond the surface, to what no one else had seen, even himself. "I know I shouldn't let myself get close to you because you'll leave soon." She dropped her gaze. "I tell myself that, but it doesn't seem to make a difference. It should, but it doesn't."

Suddenly, it was important to him that she understand why he couldn't stay. Sliding his hand from her wrist to curve around her fingers, he settled on the couch, then nudged her down beside him.

"I told you the other night that I don't have a home. I've never had one. My mother died when I was young. My father had no clue how to raise a child, and he didn't bother to find out. He sent me to boarding schools, camps. I did my time at those places, then I walked away without looking back. I'm good at walking away. I've been doing it all my life."

She nodded. "I figured that out when you told me you can put everything you need into suitcases and toss them into your airplane. You don't like roots."

"I've got no use for them. You do." Staring into the fire, he laced his fingers with hers. "You put down deep roots, Ireland. You stay in one place and you make that place a home not only for you and your child, but for any stranger who happens to come your way." He turned his head, met her gaze. "You need a man who will put down roots right beside yours."

"Eventually, that's what I want."

"I've never stayed anywhere for long. I don't know that I can stay anywhere. Or if I even want to try." He eased out a breath. "I care about you, more than I've ever cared for anyone. I don't want to hurt you. I need you to know up front that there's no future with me. It just isn't in the cards. If something happens between us, I don't want you looking back with regret. I want you to be sure."

She shoved a hand through her hair. "I thought I was. When I woke up and saw you standing beside the couch, I thought I was sure."

"You'd had a bad dream. Your face was chalk white, you were shaking. Vulnerable. You reached for me because I was the nearest safe port in the storm."

He angled his chin. "You told me you don't take intimacy lightly. If you hadn't had the dream, would you have reached for me the way you did?"

"I don't know." Her dark brows slid together. "I just don't know."

He nodded. "So, tell me about the dream."

"It was so real. I could feel the man's fingers clenched in my hair, on the back of my neck." She shook her head. "What Kade said when he was here a while ago must have brought it on. Everything was so fresh in my mind."

"Lummus was here?"

"Yes, I called him when Mr. O'Connell didn't come back."

"Come back?" Rory narrowed his eyes. "His car's parked in the lot. Yours isn't. When I drove up, I thought you were gone."

"That's right, you weren't here, so you don't know."

"I don't know what?"

Peggy slid her fingers from his and rose. "This afternoon Mr. O'Connell borrowed my station wagon because his car wouldn't start. He said he'd be gone only an hour, two at the most. That was around four o'clock."

"You haven't heard from him since?"

"No."

"Why did he need to borrow your station wagon?"

"He said he had a meeting. An important one in which he might finally get some answers about what happened to the water on Hopechest Ranch."

Rory leaned forward. "Did he say who he was meeting with? And where?"

"No, and I didn't ask." She raised a shoulder. "I called Kade around nine o'clock to get his advice on what to do. He came by and got the information he needed on my station wagon so dispatch can put something on the air tonight. He said if O'Connell doesn't show up by morning, to call him and he'll list him as a missing person and issue an APB on my car."

"That's good." Rory rose. "Did you check O'Connell's room to make sure his things are still there?"

She tilted her head. "You're thinking like Kade. We did that while he was here. As far as I can tell, all of Mr. O'Connell's belongings are still here."

"What about his work papers? Files? Any of that in his room?"

"No. But then, I've never seen any of his work when I've cleaned his room."

Rory walked to the fireplace, stared into the glowing embers. He thought about Blake having seen O'Connell's car parked at one of the hay sheds on Hopechest Ranch. Another car had been nosed deep in the shadows. A white car.

Rory retrieved his jacket off the wing chair. "I'm going out for a while, see if I can find O'Connell."

Peggy raised a brow. "Please don't do that just because he has my car. It's late, it's raining and the police are already looking for him."

Rory shrugged on his jacket, then walked to her. Because it was undoubtedly unwise to touch her, he kept his arms at his sides. "I'm pretty sure that my putting the brakes on our making love tonight, then telling you to take some time to think things through might be two of the stupidest things I've ever done. If I go upstairs to bed right now, I'm going to lie awake all night, telling myself how big an idiot I am. Trust me, it's better for my mental health to get some fresh air and keep busy for a while."

Her mouth curved. "I'm pretty sure I'm going to lie awake all night thinking. If it weren't for Samantha, I'd go with you and get some of that fresh air for myself."

He dipped his head. "Good night, Ireland."

"Good night."

He took one last look at her and thought how gorgeous she was, standing there in the fire's wavering glow. Her dark hair was a beautiful mess, her lips slightly parted, her green eyes glistening.

"Idiot," Rory muttered as he strode toward the door. "You're a flaming idiot, Sinclair."

Nine

Rory swung by Jake's Tavern to make sure Charlie O'Connell hadn't stopped off for a beer on his way back to Honeywell House. Although Peggy's black station wagon wasn't parked in the gravel lot, Rory checked inside the tavern just to make sure no one had seen O'Connell. No one had.

When Rory climbed back into his car, he turned on the engine before putting a call in to Blake to let him know about the EPA inspector's disappearing act.

"He didn't tell Peggy whom he was meeting?" Blake asked. "Or where?"

"No. All he said was that the meeting would take about an hour. Two at the most. O'Connell was either lying or he got sidetracked somewhere along the way. Peggy called Kade Lummus after O'Connell didn't show up. Lummus put the car's description on the air."

"The cops won't find O'Connell if he's having another clandestine meeting at one of my ranch's hay sheds."

"You're right."

"I'll put on some clothes and drive out to check the shed where I saw him before," Blake said. "I'll scope out a couple of other places on the ranch, too. While I'm doing that, why don't you drop by Ruby's to see if anyone has spotted O'Connell?"

Rory arched a brow while the car's engine idled and the wipers slapped rain from the windshield. "Ruby's?"

Blake chuckled. "This is your night to visit the town's hot spots, Sinclair. First Jake's, now Ruby's."

"Is Ruby's another dive?"

"Bite your tongue. Ruby's is more like the heartbeat of Prosperino. It's a café on Main Street, across from City Hall. It's *the* place where the locals go to exchange news. Some people call that gossip. Here's a tip—Ruby's meat loaf is out of this world."

"It's a little late for meat loaf."

"Then try some of Ruby's cherry pie. It's almost as good as Peggy's. Almost, but not quite."

"Yeah, thanks." Scowling, Rory clicked off his cell phone. He was trying his damnedest to keep his mind on Charlie O'Connell and off his landlady—who he could be ravishing this very moment if his conscience hadn't gotten in the way.

"Hell."

By the time Rory turned onto Main Street the rain fell in sheets, obscuring the café's wide-pane front windows in a watery blur. Only a few cars angled in the parking spots in front. Peggy's station wagon wasn't one of them.

He parked his car, then shouldered open the door against the wind and the rain. As he dashed to the sidewalk, he wondered how many more times he was destined to get wet that night.

Inside the café, the air was ripe with good, rich scents and the clatter of dishes. A long, Formica counter with the requisite stools stretched along one wall. A three-tiered stand holding homemade pies sat on one end of the counter. Tables and chairs of a serviceable metal dotted the yellowed linoleum floor. Booths covered in red vinyl lined two walls.

Rory shoved his fingers through his damp hair while his gaze swept over the smattering of customers. His chin rose when he spotted Michael Longstreet sitting with another man in a booth at the rear of the café.

"Mayor," Rory said when he reached the booth.

"Sinclair." Longstreet, clad in a starched white shirt and jeans, returned Rory's handshake, then gestured at his companion, a solidly built man with a linebacker's shoulders. "Joe Colton, meet Rory Sinclair."

"Nice to meet you, Mr. Colton." Rory's first impression of the former U.S. Senator and corporate magnate was one of vitality and health and well-channeled power. "I've heard a lot about you."

"Call me Joe, and take a load off," he said, sliding over on the bench seat to make room. The patriarch of the Colton family had a tanned, square-jawed face softened by kind blue eyes. He wore a thick sweater a shade darker than his eyes, and khaki pants. When he lifted his head, the overhead lights picked up the threads of gray in his dark hair. "You're the chemist working for Blake Fallon, right?"

"That's right." Rory pulled off his leather jacket, hung it on the back of an empty chair, then slid in beside Joe. "The mayor's making my job a lot easier by loaning me his Bonanza so I can run tests at a lab in San Francisco."

Michael shrugged, his sun-streaked brown hair skimming his shirt collar. "If you weren't flying her, she'd be on the ground all the time. With all that's going on, I haven't had a chance to think about flying."

"In case that changes, I'm not planning to take her up tomorrow," Rory said. "The tests I'm running right now take forty-eight hours for results to come back. I won't need to fly to San Francisco until the day after tomorrow."

"Fine. The plane's yours for as long as you need it."

A middle-aged waitress with expansive hips and brown hair teased into a beehive appeared beside the booth. Order pad in one hand, she nodded at Rory. "Get you something, sugar?"

"Coffee."

Joe leaned in. "Is this your first visit to Ruby's?"

"Yes."

"You should try her cherry pie."

Michael smiled. "Joe, he's staying at Peggy's place."

Joe raised an eyebrow. "Oh, well, in that case you're probably getting your fill of Peggy's desserts. Nobody can top 'em. Not even Ruby."

I wouldn't know. Rory eased out a breath. Thinking

about the gorgeous, sexy woman he had left—untouched!—at the inn had him rubbing a hand over his face. He looked at the waitress. "I'll pass on dessert. Bring me coffee. Black."

"Sure thing, sugar."

He waited to get down to business until the woman settled the steaming cup in front of him, then refilled Joe's and Michael's cups.

"Charlie O'Connell, the EPA inspector, had car trouble earlier today. He borrowed Peggy's station wagon to go to a meeting. He was due back at the inn hours ago, but hasn't made it yet. She hasn't heard from him. Have either of you seen him?"

Joe pursed his lips. "Our paths haven't crossed for a couple of days. How about you, Michael?"

"I haven't seen him today. Where was this meeting?"

"That's one of the problems—no one knows. O'Connell didn't tell Peggy where the meeting was, or who it was with. All he told her was that he had a good chance of getting some answers to what it is that contaminated the water on Hopechest Ranch."

Michael whistled softly. "We could use those answers. We *need* those answers."

"That's right," Joe agreed. "We can't do much about stopping the contamination, and preventing it from happening again, until we find out what the hell got into the water. And how the hell it got there."

"I know," Rory said. "I'm hoping to have some answers for you soon."

Joe raised a hand. "I'm not hammering at you, son. I know getting results from a lab takes time. It's just that all those kids out at Hopechest Ranch haven't had a lot of breaks in their lives. They need one now.''

A dim beeping had Michael pulling the pager off of his belt. His mouth tightened as he read the display. ''Great. Just what I need to end the day.''

''Problem?'' Joe asked.

''Homer Wentworth wants me to call him.''

Joe ducked his head. ''Glad you're the mayor and not me,'' he murmured into his coffee.

Michael looked at Rory. ''Have you met Homer?''

''No.''

''Lucky you. He's the town's malcontent. A bitter old man who doesn't like Hopechest and what he calls those good-for-nothing-kids who live there. He comes to every city council meeting just to carp over each dollar that's spent.'' Michael paused, his mouth curving into a wry grin. ''Too bad Suzanne's not here. I'd have her call the old goat.''

''Suzanne?'' Rory thought of the woman whom Peggy had said delivered the packet of toxicology reports to the inn. ''The same Suzanne who works for Blake at Hopechest?''

''Right, Suzanne Jorgenson,'' Michael replied. ''She attends all the city council meetings, too. Whenever Homer starts complaining about Hopechest, Suzanne jumps right in the middle of him. It's a pleasure to sit back and watch her duke it out verbally with Homer. The woman packs a punch.''

Rory noted the look of frank admiration that had settled in Michael's eyes when he spoke of Suzanne Jorgenson. Something there, Rory decided. Something that encompassed more than just city business.

"Guess I'll go back to my office and give Homer a call." The mayor slid out of the booth, clipped his pager back onto his belt. "Wish me luck."

"You've got it," Joe said.

Rory rose, shook Michael's hand. "Good luck. And thanks again for the use of your Bonanza."

"No problem. Good luck with those tests."

"I'll let you know as soon as I get some answers."

As the mayor strode away, Rory slid his hands into the pockets of his slacks and shifted his thoughts to Blake Fallon. To the guilt Blake felt over his father trying to kill Joe Colton. To the dread Blake felt at the prospect someone had contaminated the water on Hopechest Ranch as an attempt to revenge what Emmett Fallon had done. Now that he'd met Joe Colton, Rory figured this was a good time to start making up to Blake for his having taken their friendship for granted for so many years.

He met Joe's gaze. "Do you have time for another cup of coffee?"

"Sure."

Rory motioned for the waitress, then slid into the side of the booth Michael had vacated. After their cups were refilled, he said, "Mr. Colton—Joe—I don't just work for Blake, I'm a friend of his, too."

"That so?"

"Yes. We roomed together in college." Rory's mouth curved. "Raised a lot of hell together. Over the past years Blake and I lost touch. That's my fault. I'm not exactly an expert at maintaining ties. I never felt the need to do that. Lately I've started thinking that isn't the best thing a person can do. I plan to keep in touch with Blake from now on.''

"I imagine that will make him happy."

"I hope so. When I arrived in Prosperino, I didn't know anything about what Blake had been through the past couple of months."

"You're talking about his dad, right? About Emmett trying to kill me. Twice.''

"Yes.'' Rory sipped his coffee. "In college, whenever Blake talked about how you and your wife took him in for foster care, I always got the feeling he thought you walked on water."

"Blake got a rough deal with Emmett jumping from one marriage to the next. Meredith and I happened to be there when Blake needed a stable home environment. We had the means to give him one, so we did."

"According to Blake, you did that same thing for a lot of kids.''

Joe smiled. "Once Meredith and I got started, we didn't want to stop.''

"Blake also mentioned that you and Mrs. Colton are paying the medical expenses for everyone who drank contaminated water."

Joe raised a shoulder. "All those kids, the Hopechest staff are innocent victims. They deserve the best medical care available. It makes Meredith and myself feel good that we can give it to them."

"I know Blake appreciates all you're doing. And all you've done for him. I also know he's wondering if someone purposely contaminated the water on Hopechest as an act of revenge against him."

"Revenge?" Joe's dark brows slid together. "What sort of revenge?"

"Emmett Fallon tried to kill you. He's locked in San Quentin, so no one can get to him. Blake's out in the open at Hopechest. A target, so to speak."

"Good God." Joe's eyes widened in dawning dismay. "You think this whole thing is about revenge? That someone's gone after Blake because of what Emmett did to me?"

"I think it's possible. So does Blake."

"Christ, that never occurred to me."

"It's a theory at this point. I just don't think we should discount any scenario until we know for sure what contaminated the water and how it got there."

"I agree."

Rory didn't want to mention the list of names Blake had compiled of people who would be in a position to benefit if he lost his job at Hopechest. Or those who might be inclined to seek revenge for Emmett Fallon's attempts on the life of Prosperino's favorite citizen.

Rory knew that a lot of Joe Colton's friends and family were on that second list. So far, the background checks the FBI had run on those individuals had come back clear. He couldn't find anyone who'd had chemical or biological training in the past and might know how to contaminate a water well. No former army medics. No one who had worked for a doctor, veterinarian or pharmaceutical company. No one who even looked suspicious.

Rory shifted his gaze back to Joe. "I'm telling you this because Blake is already dealing with a lot of guilt over what Emmett did to you. If it turns out someone contaminated the water on Hopechest to get back at Blake, and innocent kids have suffered because of that, he'll take on even more guilt. I just thought you should know.''

"I appreciate that.'' Joe's mouth tightened. "I'll talk to Blake tomorrow, make sure he understands that I don't hold him accountable for what Emmett did.'' His eyes darkened to a cobalt blue. "If it turns out someone used me as an excuse to contaminate that water, they're going to have to deal with me. I'll see to it personally they have hell to pay.''

"It will be a pleasure to watch.''

Joe paused, his gaze assessing. "Seems to me, you're a lot better friend to Blake than you think you are.''

"I could have done better over the years. A lot better.''

"If you're trying to make amends, you've started out on the right track.'' Joe glanced at his watch. "It's getting late. I'd better get home to Meredith. And you're probably ready to get back to Honeywell House.''

As they climbed out of the booth, Rory thought about the hours he would spend there, lying in bed, thinking about Peggy. Wanting her.

He shook hands with Joe. "I think I'll drive around awhile and see if I have any luck finding O'Connell. I can use the fresh air.''

After he left Ruby's diner, Rory drove through the dark, rolling California countryside that bordered Prosperino. Five miles out of town, his cell phone rang. It was Blake, checking in to advise he had found no sign of O'Connell or of Peggy's station wagon anywhere on Hopechest Ranch. On impulse, Rory steered his car north on the coastal highway. By then, the rain had moved out across the ocean; he rolled down his window and listened to the angry, churning surf beat against the cliffs while cool, salty air flowed around him.

The search for O'Connell was a dead end. Not a surprise. Rory knew, without his having any idea of the EPA inspector's destination, that finding the man by chance would take a miracle.

At three o'clock in the morning, Rory pulled into the lot at the side of Honeywell House. O'Connell's rental was the only other car there. In the distance, the greenhouse squatted in the inky shadows.

The deep-seated instinct Rory had always trusted told him that something had happened to the man. Otherwise, he wouldn't have purposely disappeared. If O'Connell did have his own agenda concerning the water contamination, it made no sense for him to call attention to himself by keeping Peggy's car past the agreed time. The man wasn't stupid—he *had* to know that the cops would be looking for the station wagon by now. On the other hand, if O'Connell was on the up-and-up and got delayed by car trouble or something similar, he would have called and let Peggy know.

If he was able to call, that is.

Rory got out of his car and headed up the inn's cobblestone walk. While he walked, his mind worked, step by meticulous step, to expand the theory he'd formulated over the past hours. Whatever trouble O'Connell had stumbled into, he'd gotten there in Peggy's station wagon. That connected whatever was going on to Peggy…and Samantha. Rory didn't feel like standing around, waiting to see if that trouble found its way to Honeywell House.

He unlocked the front door, stepped into the still, silent foyer. The same lamp that had been lit hours before glowed a weak, welcoming light. As always, the air held the inviting scents of lavender, cinnamon and vanilla. Peggy's scent.

His gaze shifted toward the study, lit in silver light and shadows. The fire was out. Peggy no longer curled on the couch. He closed his eyes. Hours had passed since he'd held her, touched her, yet his desire for her had not lessened. With the inn huddled around him like a warm, soft blanket, he realized he felt a kind of wanting he had never before experienced.

"Get over it," he muttered.

Just because he wanted her naked beneath him, shuddering and helpless didn't mean that was ever going to happen. Especially now, after what he had told her about himself. He was a man with secrets, one who had allowed her to know him only on the surface, one who had no intention of staying after his job was done. He represented everything she didn't want.

As if to rid himself of the thought, he moved his shoulders with a quick, restless jerk. It was late. He had one round of business to take care of before he went to bed.

He took the stairs up to his third-floor room, stripped off his leather jacket, tossed it on the bed, then opened his field kit. He retrieved his Polaroid camera and the small, FBI-issued Kel light.

Silently, he retraced his steps along the lighted hallway and down the staircase to the second floor. As he walked, he slung the Polaroid's strap over his shoulder, then pulled a credit card from his billfold. The inn was old; the locks were the kind set into the doorknobs instead of more secure dead bolts. When he reached the door that displayed the brass 2, Rory slid the thin plastic card between the door and the jamb. In a matter of seconds, he was inside O'Connell's dark room where the faint scent of lilacs hung in the air.

Kade Lummus and Peggy had already checked to make sure O'Connell's personal property was still there. Rory knew that the cop would have conducted only a cursory search. Since he wasn't privy to Blake's suspicions about O'Connell, Lummus had no reason to suspect the man's extended absence was due to anything other than his being a jerk.

Rory's sixth sense told him different.

He swept the Kel light around the room, its beam throwing his shadow in every direction. His mouth curved when he saw that the room had the same layout as his, which made it easier to get around with only the Kel light's narrow beam. He moved soundlessly to the window, unlocked it, then eased it up. The room looked out over the parking lot. If O'Connell—or anyone else—drove up, Rory would hear the car's engine.

Turning, he crossed to the chest of drawers. Gas-station charge slips, cash-register receipts, a couple of paper clips and a few pennies were scattered across the top. Clamping the Kel light in his mouth like a cigar, he lined up the charge slips, aimed the Polaroid and snapped two pictures in quick succession. The camera's flash was a sudden, blinding strobe of light in the dark room. He repeated the process with the receipts. Rory knew the locations on the receipts and charge slips would at least give him a starting point at which to backtrack O'Connell's movements.

Rory returned the papers to their original disarray. That done, he quickly looked through the drawers, but found only clothing.

He moved to the closet, pulled open the door, patted down the shirts and jackets hanging inside, checked the pockets. Nothing. He crouched, scanned the bottom of the closet. He shook the pair of shoes sitting there, slid his fingers inside each shoe to make sure nothing was hidden inside.

He rose, closed the closet door with a soft snap, then crossed to the bed. A phone number with an area code Rory didn't recognize had been scribbled in red ink on the pad of paper beside the telephone. He shot a photo of the number.

Leaning, he lifted one edge of the bedspread and pushed his arm between the mattress and box springs. Nothing hidden there. He straightened the spread, then walked into the bathroom. There, he poked through the shaving kit sitting beside the sink. Nothing unexpected. Returning to the bedroom, Rory eased out a breath. Unless the phone number, receipts or gas-station charge slips led somewhere, he had just wasted his time. He moved to the window, lowered it, then secured the lock. One last sweep of the Kel light's beam assured him he had left the room in the same condition as when he'd entered.

Back in the lighted hallway, Rory walked to the staircase, then hesitated. Instead of taking the stairs up to his room, he stashed the camera behind a potted palm and headed downstairs.

He walked through the foyer, checked the front door to make sure he had locked it behind him. From there, he strode into the study, then headed toward the rear of the inn.

The kitchen was dark. The refrigerator's soft hum filled the air that held a vague, spicy scent. He tried the knob on the back door, found it locked and secure. Silently, he walked to the entrance of the dark hallway that led to Peggy and Samantha's rooms, paused there.

Something inside his chest tightened and he felt a pull to both the woman and the child. To the inn. For the first time in his adult memory he didn't know what he wanted himself. For himself.

Immediately, he quelled the feeling. Jaw set, he turned, walked away. Those thoughts were too new, too confusing to try to make sense of. Maybe after he finished the job he had come here to do, he would consider those feelings. Try to sort them out. Deal with them.

Now wasn't the time.

Ten

"**M**omma, you're sure you won't forget to take my sleeping bag to Gracie's while I'm at school? 'N' my backpack, too?"

"I'm not likely to forget," Peggy said as Samantha squirmed beside her on the couch in the sitting area just off their bedrooms. "You've already reminded me twenty times this morning that I need to drop off your things at Gracie's house. Now hold still so I can finish braiding your hair."

"Be sure 'n' get my art kit, too. It's in the car."

"Yes, I know."

If only Mr. O'Connell had brought back the car. Peggy frowned as she put the finishing touches on the neat French braid that subdued Samantha's dark gypsy curls. She had hoped that when she got up this morning, her station wagon would be parked in the lot near

the back door. It wasn't. She had taken her passkey
and checked Charlie O'Connell's room, just to make
sure he hadn't gotten a ride back to the inn sometime
during the night. He hadn't. As much as she disliked
the man, she couldn't help but fear that something bad
had happened to him. And to her station wagon.

Samantha fidgeted around to face her. "Be sure
Bugs and Bugsy are still in my backpack."

"Enough, Samantha. I promise you your things will
get to Gracie's house in time for tonight's slumber
party. Now, change the subject."

Samantha's lower lip poked out and she expelled a
huff. "Soooorrry." She gazed up through a fan of impossibly thick, dark lashes. "Are you mad at me,
Momma?"

Peggy put a hand to her right temple where a drum
was beginning to beat. Her missing station wagon
wasn't the only reason for her strained temper. With
her system churning from last night's encounter with
Rory, she had gotten very little sleep. It was no wonder.
First, she had thrown herself at him. He'd fended off
her advances while outlining the reasons she shouldn't
want him. Then he'd shifted gears, telling her *he*
wanted *her,* and had left the decision up to her of
whether they would ever make love.

Heaven knew she wanted to. Just thinking about the
feel of his hands on her flesh, the way his mouth fit so
perfectly against hers sent heat surging into her belly.
She just didn't know if sleeping with him was the right
thing to do. No matter what they shared, no matter
what happened during their time together, he would

leave. Walk away. She knew she couldn't watch him go and feel nothing.

That cold realization had kept her awake most of the night. She hadn't tossed and turned so much as lain, staring up at the ceiling. Logic told her she should pass on stepping into intimacy with him, reminded her that he wasn't a man she could have for keeps. It was the stirring in her heart that pulled her to him.

"Momma?"

With the thin, slatted window blinds half-open, the first sunlight the region had seen in weeks flooded into the room, illuminating Samantha's pixie face.

"No, sweetheart, I'm not mad at you." Peggy dropped a kiss on her daughter's pouty lips. "I just have a lot of things on my mind." Smiling, she skimmed her knuckles against a baby-soft cheek. "One of those things is making sure you don't miss the van to preschool."

"But I never miss the van."

"True." Peggy snagged the traffic-stopping red bow that matched Samantha's corduroy jumper off the coffee table in front of the couch. Without her station wagon, there was no way she could manage to get Samantha to preschool on time if she missed the van. "I don't want today to be a first." With the ease of experience, Peggy deftly secured the bow at the base of the braid.

Just then, a light rap sounded on the door that led to the hallway.

"I'll get it!" Sliding off the couch, Samantha dashed to the door, pulled it open. She beamed a smile as sweet as the sunshine glowing outside the windows. "Mr. Rory!"

"Good morning, angel-face." Smiling, he tweaked her nose, then shifted his killer-blue gaze to Peggy. "Morning, Ireland."

"Good morning." Just the sight of him tightened her throat. He was wearing a houndstooth-check shirt, khaki slacks and loafers. The neck of the shirt was unbuttoned. At the V below his throat, she saw the beginnings of dark chest hairs. She remembered the look of that hard-planed chest, the muscled shoulders. Her fingers curled against an itch to touch; the drumming in her heart matched the rhythm in her temple.

"I'm sorry to interrupt." His gaze flicked down to Samantha, then back up. "I checked the lot and wondered if you got a call during the night from anyone?"

"No, I haven't heard a word. Nothing."

"Mr. Rory, guess where I get to go tonight?" Samantha slipped her small hand into his and tugged him a few steps into the room. "Guess!"

He bent down, an expression of deep concentration on his face. "Hmm, let me think. To the carrot patch with Bugs and Bugsy?"

Samantha rolled her eyes. "No, to Gracie's. It's her birthday." Excitement had her bouncing on her heels. "We're gonna see a movie 'n' eat pizza 'n' stay up all night."

"Wow, all night?"

"Yeah, Momma said I could. But I have to have Bugs and Bugsy in bed by eleven."

"That sounds about right."

"Momma's gonna bring my sleeping bag 'n' back-pack to Gracie's. 'N' my art kit, too. It's in the car."

Rory flicked Peggy a look over Samantha's shoulder. "Sounds like you'll have everything you need for a night away from home."

"Yeah. 'N' when I have my birthday in May, I get to have a slumber party, too. Momma promised."

"Then I guess you'll have one."

From outside came two short, sharp blasts of a horn.

Peggy laid Samantha's hairbrush aside and rose off the couch. "That's the van for preschool."

"Bye, Mr. Rory!"

When Samantha lunged into Rory's arms and hugged his neck, Peggy closed her eyes. *She* wasn't going to be the only person dealing with disappointment when he left Prosperino.

"Bye, angel-face."

Samantha raced down the hallway into the kitchen, Peggy following. Although Rory moved with his usual ghostlike silence, she sensed him trailing behind her. She glanced across her shoulder, saw she was right.

"Help yourself to some coffee," she told him as she bundled Samantha into her powder-blue thermal jacket. "The mugs are by the coffeemaker."

"Thanks."

She ushered Samantha out the back door. "Have a good time tonight. I love you," Peggy added as her daughter sprang down the porch steps with the easy grace of youth.

"Love you, too!"

Peggy waited until the van disappeared down the road, then walked back inside, closing the kitchen door behind her. Rory leaned one hip against the center island while he sipped from a mug of steaming coffee. He looked so at home, she thought. Like he belonged.

She shook her head. He didn't belong, she reminded herself. Didn't *want* to belong.

"Samantha is a ball of energy," he observed. "Do you ever have trouble keeping up?"

"Sometimes it's a challenge." She smiled. "But never a hardship. Samantha is the best thing in my life."

"She's beautiful, Ireland," he said, his voice quiet and soft. "Except for the eye color, she looks just like you."

"Thanks." Peggy slid her palms down the front of her black slacks. "I'm sorry I don't have breakfast ready. This is the first time in days that you haven't left the inn before dawn."

"It's my fault for not telling you I'd be here. I don't need to go into the lab today. I have some things to check out around town this morning." He sipped his coffee, his blue eyes tracking her over the mug's rim as she moved to the side of the island opposite him. "Have you called Lummus yet to let him know O'Connell hasn't made it back?"

"No, I wanted to get Samantha off first."

"I'll call him if you want me to."

"Yes, please." Her forehead creased. "I've been thinking about how Mr. O'Connell acted when he asked to borrow the station wagon."

"And?"

"I saw nothing in his demeanor that made me think

he wouldn't have it back on time. I'm afraid something has happened to him. Something bad.''

"I think so, too. It's just a feeling, but I can't shake it.''

"How late did you stay out last night looking for him?''

"Make that this morning. I got back here around three.''

With the sunlight streaming through the kitchen windows she saw the lines of fatigue at the corners of his eyes. "I'm sorry you lost sleep on account of one of my other guests.''

"O'Connell wasn't the only reason," he said, his gaze holding hers. "I needed some fresh air, too.''

The muscles in her stomach tightened so quickly that she nearly winced. "I know.''

She didn't need a reminder of what had happened between them last night. Or, to be more exact, what *hadn't* happened. As it was, every nerve in her body was in a scrambling process that came from being in the same room with the man.

She turned to the refrigerator, its door awash with Samantha's crayon drawings. "How does caramel apple French toast sound?" she asked over her shoulder. "With a side of bacon?''

"Like heaven." He walked to the coffeemaker, refilled his mug. "Do you know how many men in this town rave about the desserts you bake?''

"Actually, they're my grandmother's desserts," Peggy said across her shoulder as she pulled items out of the refrigerator. "Nearly all the recipes I use are Gran's. I inherited them, along with the inn." With her arms cradling a carton of eggs, milk, a package of bacon and the container that held her homemade caramel apple topping, Peggy used a hip to shove the door closed. "You might rave, too, if you ever let me keep my end of our bargain and make you dessert."

"Speaking of that, I tested the inn's water before I came down this morning. It's still fine."

"Good. That's good to hear."

"Do you have a straight-line number to the police station for Lummus?"

Peggy blinked at the sudden change of subject. "Yes." She pulled a heavy mixing bowl from under the island. "It's on a card in the drawer nearest the phone."

While Rory placed the call, she put the topping on to heat and laid slices of bacon in a skillet. That done, she pulled a loaf of fresh-baked bread from the storage bin and began slicing off thick pieces. In minutes, the kitchen warmed with the scents of baking.

After ending his call, Rory slid onto one of the long-legged stools at the island. "Lummus will have dispatch broadcast your station wagon as stolen. That way, it'll go into the nationwide computer. If a cop anywhere in the country stops the car and runs it, he'll get a hit. You should call your insurance company and let them know what's going on."

"You're right. I'll do that as soon as I'm finished here."

"Lummus is also upgrading O'Connell's status to wanted-in-questioning-for-auto-theft. That way, if he gets stopped, the cops can do more than question him.

They can hold him. The fact that he's a missing person isn't against the law.''

Peggy wrinkled her brow. "I hope he doesn't get upgraded to anything worse."

"Me, either. When he checked into the inn, you had O'Connell fill out a registration card, right?"

Nodding, she used a long fork to nudge the bacon strips around the skillet. "Yes. The same type of card you filled out."

"Lummus asked me to call him back and give him the home address O'Connell listed. And the phone number for his office."

"I'll get the card for you."

"You're busy. If you'll tell me where it is, I'll get it."

"In the registration desk. Top left-hand drawer."

Instead of heading that way, Rory rested his forearms on the island and leaned in.

"Something else?" she asked.

"Yes. I'm wondering about Samantha's things for the slumber party."

"What about them?"

"How do you plan to get them to Gracie's house?"

Peggy blew out a breath. "I have that all worked out. The town mechanic keeps a loaner car at his garage for when someone has to leave their car for repair and they don't have access to another one. I'm going to call him as soon as he opens and see if I can rent the loaner."

"You could hold off on doing that for a couple of days. Like I said, I have some places I need to go this morning, but I should be back early this afternoon. I plan to shut myself in my room and catch up on paperwork the rest of the day. While I'm doing that, you can use my rental car.''

''I appreciate that.'' She paused. ''I have other errands I have to run, too. And the marketing to do.''

Rory glanced at the bowl of batter in which she was whisking eggs and milk into a froth. A smile crept around his mouth. ''I'm the last person who wants you to run out of food. If you can manage to get away from here for a while early in the morning, you can drive me to the airport and drop me off. That way you'll have the car all day tomorrow, too. I can call and let you know when you need to be back at the airport to pick me up.''

''Thanks.'' She moved the bacon from the skillet to a platter, then slid it into the warming drawer. ''Your sharing your car with me is a lot of trouble for you.''

''O'Connell taking your station wagon has caused you trouble. I'm trying to even things out.'' He slid off the stool. ''I'll get his registration card and give Lummus a call back.''

''Okay.'' A lump formed in Peggy's throat as she watched Rory walk out the door then disappear down the hallway. She could no longer deny that, in her entire life, she had never wanted a man so badly. Not even Jay.

She pulled her bottom lip between her teeth. What, she wondered, was she going to do about Rory Sinclair?

It wasn't a bad evening by coastal standards, Peggy thought as she stood four stories up on the inn's narrow widow's walk. Clouds had drifted in late that afternoon, blocking the sun, promising more rain later on. But the fog bank that had been so constant lately was nothing more than wisps as evening turned to night.

Minutes ago, the moon had started to rise, tinting the landscape in silver light. Leaning a hip against the sturdy wood rail, Peggy tucked her hands into the pockets of her trench coat and hunched her shoulders against the advancing chill.

With the inn snuggled high on the hillside, she had an unobstructed view of a section of stark, barren cliffs and, beyond them, the sea. As she watched, wave swallowed churning wave, frothing like champagne against the rugged rocks.

Her thoughts were just as restless.

All day she had continued to struggle with the question of what to do about Rory. She had mulled things over while she drove his car to drop Samantha's things by Gracie's house, swung by the cleaners and after that the market. Although she knew the spur-of-the-moment purchase she'd made at the upscale boutique wedged between two art galleries was her subconscious registering its vote, the logical part of her brain still had made no decision as to whether she wanted to take their relationship further.

At least she didn't think so.

She scowled. It would probably help if she could figure out how she felt about the man. But her system was too unsettled. Too many emotions were battering inside her to allow her to see, as she wanted, the right direction to take. All she knew was that she wanted. Badly.

"Ireland?"

Jolting at the sound of Rory's voice, she turned, thinking she would never get used to the silent way he moved. Since he had changed into a black sweater and gray slacks, she assumed he was planning on going somewhere. That, she thought, would take care of her having to make a decision about whether the rest of her evening would be spent in his company. Soaking in a hot tub while starting the paperback she'd picked up at the market would be a much safer route to take.

She slid her hands into the pockets of her coat. "Thanks for the use of your car. The keys are by the phone in the kitchen."

"I was on my way downstairs when I noticed the door leading up here was open." He angled his chin. "The inn is as still as a tomb tonight."

"Things are quiet," she agreed. "That's to be expected. January and February are my slowest months. I don't have any reservations on the book for another couple of weeks." The wind gusted, picking up strands of her hair. She skimmed them back from her cheek. "Some friends who own one of the art galleries in town called and offered me the use of their house at Lake Tahoe. I think I'll take Samantha there for a vacation after you check out."

"That shouldn't be much longer." He shifted his gaze to the south where the lights of Prosperino glowed in the advancing twilight. "You've got quite a view."

"Yes. Gran and I used to sit out here and count the stars. Samantha and I have carried on the family tradition."

Rory glanced up. "Since there aren't any stars out

yet, I have to figure you're standing here wondering what happened to O'Connell and your station wagon."

"Among other things."

Rory took a step forward, placed his hands on the rail. "I never used to take time to look at the scenery. Never cared about looking. Lately I'm finding myself doing a lot of that. I haven't figured out why."

"You miss a lot of beautiful things when you don't bother to stand in one place and take in what's around you."

He turned toward her, his face nearly lost in the twilight shadows. "You're right about that. What other things?"

She raised a brow. "What?"

"You said you're thinking about O'Connell, among other things. What other things?"

She dragged in an uneven breath. It was now or never. "You. I was thinking about you."

"What about me?"

"I was trying to decide if I should come downstairs and knock on the door to your room. Since you're going out, you've saved me from having to make that decision."

His eyes turned intense. "What if I wasn't going out? What would your decision be?"

"I don't have a clue. That's why I'm still up here."

"Think you'll make up your mind anytime soon?"

"Hard to say." She pulled her gaze from his and stared at the endless expanse of ocean. "I keep telling myself to be sensible. To remember what you said last night. That there are things about you that you can't, won't, tell me. That you're leaving as soon as your job here is done. That you're not the right man for me.''

"None of that has changed."

"I know." Inside her pockets, her hands clenched. "It doesn't seem to matter."

He took a step toward her. "It should matter, Ireland. It *does* matter."

"Maybe. Probably." Shaking her head, she turned to face him. "I don't know what to feel around you, Rory. To tell you the truth, I don't know if I can handle knowing what I feel."

The next step he took put him an inch from her. She could smell the mix of soap and spicy cologne that clung to his skin. He reached, ran his hands up the sleeves of her coat to her shoulders, then down to her elbows again. "If it helps, I don't know what I feel around you, either."

She gazed up, his blue eyes looking like smoke in the advancing darkness. "Then I guess we're both confused on that point."

"Sounds like it."

"I don't know how it's possible to have been swept away so quickly. To want so desperately what I know I shouldn't have." As she spoke, she placed a palm against his chest, felt the heat from his body, the beat of his heart.

A wave of unspeakable need fired through her blood.

In that slash of time, the decision was made. She no longer had the will to fight whatever was growing inside of her. She didn't want to spend her life regretting what might have been. Rory was here. In her life now. She didn't care if she never saw him again. Didn't want to wonder if there could be more between them if their lives were linked by more than just a physical need. She wanted the now. Him.

She reached up with her fingertips and traced the deep curve of his bottom lip while the muscles in her stomach clenched. "Last night you held me at arm's length. If I tell you that I want you, that I want us, are you going to do the same thing tonight?"

"I wish to hell I could. I *should*. Problem is, I'm not strong enough to do that twice in one lifetime." His voice had gone low and raw. "All I can manage right now is to ask if you're sure."

"Yes." She rose on tiptoe, her body sliding up, pressing against his as she placed a soft kiss against the corner of his mouth. "I'm sure."

In the next instant his arm wrapped around her waist, lashing her to him. His fingers shot into her hair, arching her head back as his mouth settled on hers. The kiss was hard, explosive, searing.

Desire flooded her veins like flame leaping along spilled gasoline.

Desperate to feel him, she shoved up his sweater, fumbled open the buttons of his shirt. Her fingers slid across the whipcord strength of his chest, the crisp mat of hair. She pulled her mouth from his, used her lips and tongue on his nipple. She felt the quick contraction of his muscles, the jump in his heartbeat.

He knotted his fingers in her hair and drew her face up. "You do that, and this isn't going to take long at all." His lips grazed her temple, her cheek, the curve of her jaw. "Slow down, Ireland." When his teeth grazed her throat, her knees began to tremble. "I want slow. I want this to take all night."

"Yes," she breathed. Her pulse throbbed with a primitive beat. "All night."

Just then, the floodlights set into the landscaping below switched on automatically. The face of the inn illuminated in a fan of bright light.

"Dammit, I don't want the entire town for an audience," Rory grated against her throat.

"Downstairs," she urged breathlessly. One of her hands was locked on the back of his neck; the other was still beneath his sweater, inside his shirt, against his chest. "We have to go downstairs. Now."

"We're going." His mouth continued to plunder her throat as he tugged her toward the door. Together, they stumbled down the short staircase, arms and legs banging against the banister, the wall, the doorjamb. When they surged into the dimly lit hallway, Rory shoved the door closed then pressed her back against it.

"Your place, or mine?" he asked while his deft fingers loosened the belt on her coat.

Lungs heaving, Peggy slid her gaze sideways. The door to his room was at the end of the hallway. Hers was down two flights of stairs, through the foyer, study and the kitchen. She wasn't sure they could make it that far. In her hazy brain she confirmed that she had her cell phone clipped to her coat pocket in case Samantha needed her during the night.

"Your room. It's closer. A lot."

"I was hoping you'd say that." Belt loosened, he shoved back the coat's flaps. His eyes sparked; for an instant he went still as stone. "If I'd known sooner this was all you had on underneath this coat..."

Her pulse throbbed harder when his hungry gaze raked over the thin chemise of ivory silk. "I bought this today when I made an unscheduled stop at a boutique in town. Going there was out of my way. I wasted your gas."

"You can borrow my car every day if you make stops like that." He shoved the coat off her shoulders, nudged it down to her elbows while he replaced fabric with teeth. "Hell, you can have the damn car."

"It's a rental."

"Yeah. Right."

With their mouths locked together, they staggered down the hallway. Somehow, she wound up facing him, stumbling backward when the coat's dangling belt wrapped around one of her ankles. Rory's hands curved over her backside, lifted her. She wrapped her legs around his waist and used her teeth on his throat.

At the door to his room, he muttered a curse when he jerked at the knob, found it locked. By the time he dug the key out of his pocket, managed to slide it into the lock and pull open the door, she had his sweater off.

He slammed the door behind them, locked it. She kicked off her slippers, fought the coat off of her arms while nipping at his bottom lip.

The room was dark, lit only by slashes of silver moonlight. With her clinging to him like a silken burr, he went down on his knees. One of his hands cupped her head as he laid her back onto the braided rug that pooled in the center of the bedroom. Shoving the chemise up to her waist, he knelt between her spread thighs, his shirt hanging open, his eyes glinting as he gazed down at her. "I was wrong." His palms cupped her silk-covered breasts. "I want fast. This first time, I want fast."

"Yes." She didn't want soft words or slow hands. Not now, not when her body ached so fiercely that she shook from it. She surged up, pushed the unbuttoned shirt down his arms, then off. Her greedy fingers went to his belt, fumbling, tugging. Seconds later, he was naked. In the moonlight, his body was beautiful, strong, with sinews that rippled and tightened as he moved.

When she reached for him again, wanting what her body so violently craved, he pushed her backward to the floor, then quickly stripped her of the thin silk. She felt a small thrill as she lay naked beneath his gaze while greed glinted in his eyes. This, then, was that dangerous man she had glimpsed the night she had looked up and found him in the foyer, watching her in silence. He knew exactly what he wanted to do to her, and all she could do was let him do it.

Leaning over her, he dipped his head, feasted on one nipple, then the other as if he were ravenous, using his teeth, his tongue, his lips. Heat saturated her, as though a furnace door had been thrown open, and the roaring blaze had enveloped her flesh.

Her hands raked along his back, her nails digging into his heated flesh. The air around them went as thick and heavy as velvet. An ache spread from deep in her center, her bones throbbing with it.

As he continued to suckle, she could hear his breath, ragged and strained against her skin.

One of his hands slid down her rib cage to her belly, along the flare of her hip, then eased lower, cupping where her flesh was hot and wet. When his fingers plunged into her, a hoarse, shuddering breath strangled in her throat.

His mouth fed at her breasts while his fingers thrust inside her with deep, grinding, glorious pleasure. She could feel every pulse beat, hundreds of them, pounding beneath her flesh. The muscles in her stomach jumped and quivered. His thumb circled the bud between her thighs, an erotic massage against her throbbing, swelling flesh.

Moaning his name, she slid her calf along his naked flank.

His fingers withdrew, entered her again, then again; the pleasure he released in her was like the rush of some wonderful drug. Sweat slicked her flesh as she felt herself going up, soaring in the fire, impaled on the wings of its heat. The climax exploded around her hard and fast. Tension drained out of her in a long shudder of ecstasy.

"Again," he murmured. His fingers continued moving inside her, his thumb massaging her flesh, shooting her back up that slippery, heated path. The second climax ripped through her, more shattering than the first.

With no strength left in her body, her hands slid from his back. Her eyes fluttered shut while he shifted, mounted her, his weight crushing her breathlessly. She felt the sweat on his skin, his muscles tight with urgency.

"Look at me. Look at me, Ireland."

With her remaining strength, she forced her eyes

open. His face was intent, his eyes staring deep into
hers as he thrust inside her, mating, possessing.

"I want to see your eyes while I take you."

He moved inside her with increasing urgency, flood-
ing her with a swelling pleasure that grew and spread.
Her mind clouded, her vision dimmed as her hips
moved like lightning, meeting him thrust for thrust, her
body arching in surrender. She felt her inner muscles
clench around him at the same time his arms tightened
around her and his body convulsed. He buried his face
against her throat and groaned her name.

Together, they slid into hot, sweet oblivion.

They made love twice more on the floor. Later Rory
found the strength to carry her to his bed. Now, with
moonlight slanting through the curtains, he leaned back
against the headboard, watching Peggy sleep. She lay
on her stomach, her head turned toward him, one arm
thrown across his stomach, her hair spreading like a
pool of ink against the white pillowcase. The dark fan
of her lashes against her cheeks made her skin look
almost translucent.

The scent of their passion hung in the cool, still air.

To please himself, he stroked a hand down her back,
over the swell of her hip. She didn't stir.

He had been drawn to other women, but never for
the long haul. Certainly he had never felt such warmth
and need as he did at this moment. Just for a heartbeat,
he wondered what it would be like to spend the rest of
his life with this one soft, sexy, beautiful woman.

His brow knit. He cared for her more than he had
cared for anyone before, he accepted that. But how he

felt about her didn't change who he was, what he was. He had spent years on his own, needing no one. What had happened between them didn't change who he was.

Who he was. He skimmed a hand over the dark pool of her hair. He felt no guilt, not with her lying beside him, not while the memory of what they had shared was so new, so potent. Somehow tonight—this one night—a cloak of sensation had settled around them, allowing him to do as he wanted without hesitation or regret.

That would all change in the morning.

He scrubbed a hand across his face, then eased out of bed. Silently, he moved to the window, used the edge of his hand to slice back one side of the curtain, and looked out toward the sea. The moon was still high, cutting a distant swath of light across the black water.

His mind spun back to the night Peggy told him about Jay Honeywell's line-of-duty death. The determination that had settled in her eyes, her voice when she vowed to never involve herself with another cop would live forever in Rory's memory.

And his conscience.

His fingers clenched on the curtain. Knowing how she felt, he had made an effort to stay away, to avoid what had happened between them tonight. That wasn't an excuse—there wasn't one. In the end, he hadn't been strong enough to be noble, hadn't been good enough to do the right thing. He'd been a man caught in a web of desire and, for the first time in his life, he hadn't walked away. He had stayed, and taken what he wanted.

He would have to deal with the consequences of his actions if Peggy found out he carried a badge.

He closed his eyes. There was no *if*. When. Limits existed to what he could and would give to her. To anyone. But he owed her the truth about himself. She deserved that. Just as he deserved to answer for what he'd done.

In the morning, he decided. He crossed back to the bed, slid in beside her, drew the covers over their naked bodies and took her in his arms. He would tell her the truth first thing in the morning.

Eleven

With a slow stretch, Peggy woke to the soft thrum of rain against the windows. It wasn't the panes in her own bedroom that the first watery rays of dawn crept through. Her mouth curved in sleepy contentment at the realization. The windows were on the inn's third floor. Rory's bedroom.

Turning her head, she gazed at the man who immediately consumed her thoughts. He lay sprawled facedown beside her, one arm draped across her waist. His head was angled toward the windows so that in the dim light she could make out the slash of one cheekbone. Against the white sheet, his face was tanned, his jaw shadowed by dark stubble.

Twin surges of contentment and desire swam through her. With a fingertip, she nudged the raven hair off his forehead. The small movement brought the

awareness of an ache, dull and sweet, through her entire body, a reminder of their long night of lovemaking.
Lying beside him, with the sound of his steady
breathing mixed with the patter of rain, she was filled
with a swirling mix of emotion.

If he was so wrong for her as he claimed, how come
he felt so right? Why had her heart reached out to this
man, this one man, when it had lain dormant for so
long?

He was so alone, she thought. Rory had no family
to speak of, no real place that he belonged. He didn't
even know the simple pleasure of coming home to his
own house, his own bed and the familiar view out his
own window.

He didn't want to know.

She closed her eyes on a soft sigh. That they had
such differences in their basic needs didn't matter. Nor
did the sobering knowledge that he would soon walk
away. What mattered was that they enjoy the remaining
time they had together.

It was then, in the quiet, still light of dawn, that she
realized what she had not known until that moment.
She didn't simply want him, need him. She loved him.
Not just for the searing-hot kisses that had made her
half-crazed, or the electric feel of his hands on her
flesh. She had fallen in love with the man beneath.
With his heart, the innate kindness, the nurturing side
he refused to acknowledge. The man who went out of
his way to bring a child a fuzzy, pink rabbit. The man
who had swept her to safety and cared for her after
she'd been attacked, then served her guests a cheese
plate. The man concerned enough to offer his car so

her daughter's treasured belongings would arrive at a slumber party.

Rising on one elbow, Peggy shoved her tumbled hair out of her eyes. Her feelings were so new, so sudden, so jumbled. She needed time to think. To adjust. Accept that she was in love with a man who would soon leave and might never come back.

Rory had to go, she knew. Just as she had to stay.

She had no choice but to deal with his absence, she resolved. Live with it. He had told her up-front that was the way things would be. Yet, she'd willingly stepped into the fire. She had lost one man she loved, and she had survived. She would do so again.

She had Samantha and she had the inn. Raising her daughter and operating a business kept her steady, maintained her balance. Last night had changed nothing about those aspects of her life.

Slowly, Peggy slipped from beneath Rory's arm. He muttered a few unintelligible words, then turned his head and buried his face in the pillow.

The rain had put a chill in the air, sending goose bumps prickling over her skin. A hard, quick throbbing of her pulse accompanied the goose bumps when she spied the pile of pale ivory silk in the center of the braided rug. She could still feel Rory's hands stripping her of the cool fabric.

Blowing out a breath, Peggy gathered up the chemise, then walked soundlessly toward the door. There, she plucked her coat off the floor and slid it on. Closing the bedroom door behind her, she padded along the dim hallway, down the three flights of stairs, then into the foyer. She paused to turn off the light she left glowing each night. That done, she headed toward the kitchen.

While she readied the coffeemaker, she glanced out the window. Any hopes she had that Charlie O'Connell might have returned overnight with her station wagon faded when she saw through the drizzling rain that Rory's car was the only one in the lot.

She opened the refrigerator, her mind formulating a breakfast menu of ham and egg blossoms with hollandaise, accented with fresh dill. The dill she would have to gather from her greenhouse. Fine, she told herself as she closed the refrigerator door with a snap. Since the attack she had avoided the greenhouse, had halted her daily routine of checking on her plants. The delicate buds she had planted in peat pots the previous week needed water and care, or she would lose them. Kade had put extra police patrols on the inn. The drifter who had probably attacked her was no longer in the area. She had to start back working in the greenhouse and today was as good a time as any.

With her emotions in such upheaval, she needed the comfort of her routine.

She turned the oven to preheat, made sure the coffeemaker had begun spewing out its heady brew, then moved down the hallway to her living quarters. She wasn't sure what time Rory would leave for the lab in San Francisco, but she wanted to make sure he had a good breakfast before he went. Since he'd been asleep when she left his room only moments ago, she estimated she had just enough time to take a quick shower, dress and collect the dill before she started cooking.

* * *

Rory felt an instant flare of disappointment when he strode into the empty kitchen where the rich scent of coffee filled the air. Dammit, he had wanted Peggy to be there, wanted her to gaze across the center island at him with those beautiful green eyes. Eyes that had gone dark and smoky throughout the long night when he had made her his.

On his way to the coffeemaker, he nudged up the sleeve of his sweater, checked his watch and winced. He should be airborne by now, halfway to the lab in San Francisco. He hadn't planned on oversleeping, hadn't planned on having a reason to have overslept.

Hadn't known he would need time to tell Peggy that she had spent the night making love with a man who carried a badge.

He shoved a hand through his hair, still damp from his hurried shower. Pouring coffee into a mug, he tried to ignore the sweaty fist of dread that lodged in his stomach. He'd had several casual affairs that had lasted over weeks, months sometimes. Never had he given thought to what he would do, how he would feel if any of the women he'd been involved with had ended the relationship before he was ready to move on. Now that prospect had panic sneaking up to scrape at the back of his throat.

He didn't want to leave the woman, the child, the inn. Not now. Not yet.

The sound of heavy footsteps on the back porch had him swinging around. Kade Lummus pushed open the door and stepped in, his uniform neat and trim, his dark hair damp, his expression grim.

Rory set his coffee aside. He had checked the parking lot from a window before coming downstairs, so he knew O'Connell hadn't returned during the night with Peggy's station wagon. "Do you have some word on O'Connell?"

"More than just some word. We found him."

"Where is he?"

Lummus stepped to the coffeemaker, filled a mug. His gaze swept the kitchen. "Where's Peggy?"

"I just came downstairs, so I'm not sure." Rory glanced across his shoulder toward the dim hallway that led off the rear of the kitchen. "Back in her room, maybe."

Lummus leaned against the counter, sipped his coffee. "O'Connell's dead. He went over a cliff in Peggy's station wagon."

"Christ." Rory had not liked the man, but he hadn't wished him dead, either. "Where?"

"North, about twenty miles from here. The road runs along the top of a cliff and is a nightmare of twists and turns. No guardrails. A county survey crew went out there this morning and saw the station wagon. Good thing, because it's hidden from the road. If it weren't for that crew, there's no telling how long it would have been until someone stumbled across the wreck."

"Any idea what happened?"

"The only thing we have right now are skid marks from two vehicles on the road at the same point the wagon went over the cliff. There's no way to tell how long those skid marks have been there, or if they were made at the same time."

"What about point of impact?"

Lummus narrowed his eyes. "There isn't one on any of the rocks or trees, so it's not like O'Connell hit a wet spot, then skidded into something and bounced over the cliff. It looks like he just headed toward the edge and went straight over."

"That could mean a car came from behind and pushed the station wagon off the road. A heavier car or truck with more power."

"Could." Rory felt Lummus's assessing scrutiny as the cop sipped his coffee. "No way to prove that."

"What about damage to the station wagon, other than what was caused by the plunge off the cliff? Any paint on it that doesn't belong?"

"There's some white paint on the right rear bumper. That's one of the reasons I'm here. I need to find out from Peggy if the paint was there before."

Rory set his jaw. "She gets attacked in her greenhouse, then it's possible someone purposely runs her station wagon off the road. All that within a few days. Do you think that's a coincidence?"

"I'm a cop, Sinclair. I don't believe in coincidence."

"Neither do I. That means someone could have thought it was Peggy behind the wheel instead of O'Connell."

"I agree."

Rory paced toward the back door, turned and stalked back to the center island. That so many questions remained unanswered in his mind had his hands balling into fists of frustration. "Is there anyone in town with a reason to hurt her? Anyone who might even try to kill her?"

"Not that I know of. You can be sure I'm keeping

my eyes open." Lummus raised a dark brow. "What about O'Connell?"

"What about him?"

"Do you know of a reason someone might want to force him off that cliff?"

"Nothing solid. Did you find any of his work papers in the car with him?"

"No."

Rory muttered an oath. "The more time that's passed without his coming up with what contaminated the water at Hopechest, the more I suspect him of holding back. And for reasons other than his being a disgruntled government worker." Rory thought about the gas-station charge slips and cash-register receipts he had photographed in O'Connell's room. Yesterday he'd checked all the locations on the receipts, asking questions about the EPA inspector, trying to dig up something—anything. He'd hit a dead end.

"Problem is," Rory added, "I have no proof that O'Connell was up to anything. I haven't exactly come up with answers about the water, either."

Lummus sat his mug on the counter, then crossed his arms over his chest. "I'm not a scientist, so I'll leave the water issue up to you."

"Fine." Rory paused. "Any idea how long O'Connell's been dead?"

"The M.E.'s aide estimated at least a day. The body's on the way to the morgue. The M.E. says he'll finish the autopsy by late afternoon, so we'll know more then."

"Has the station wagon been moved?"

"Not yet. The only way to get to the base of the

cliff is by a narrow footpath. A wrecker alone can't handle the job of getting the wagon out. We're bringing in a crane to lift it up onto the road. It'll be a couple of hours at least before the crane gets there."

"I want to take a look at the scene."

"Sorry, it's a possible crime scene. No civilians allowed."

"Dammit, Lummus, I'm not a civilian. I think you've pretty well figured that out by the questions I'm asking."

"Maybe." Lummus angled his chin. "Got some ID?"

As he walked across the kitchen, Rory glanced down the dim hallway that led to Peggy's room. It was empty. Reaching into his back pocket, he pulled out his badge case, flipped it open. "FBI special agent. I work out of the lab in D.C. That good enough to get me onto the scene?"

"I'd say so."

"FBI?"

Rory's heart stopped at the sound of Peggy's voice coming from behind him. With the air clogging in his lungs, he slowly turned.

She stood in the open doorway between the wind and the warmth, dressed in an emerald sweater and slacks. Her dark hair was pulled back from her deathly pale face, her eyes wide and dark with hurt. In the crook of one arm, she cradled a cardboard box. On top of the box lay a cutting from a plant Rory couldn't identify. She had been outside, he realized, had opened the back door and stepped into the kitchen without his hearing.

"Ireland—"

"You're an FBI agent? A cop?"

He drew a careful breath at her cool tone. "Yes."

"In that case, Agent Sinclair, I suppose this box should go to you."

Rory's gut knotted at her use of his rank. "Peggy—"

"I found it in the greenhouse, hidden behind a bag of peat moss." She rapped a finger on the shoe box. "It has Mr. O'Connell's name on it and glass vials inside. I can't imagine why he hid this in my greenhouse."

Walking stiffly to the nearest counter, she sat the box on top, then turned, the plant's cutting clenched in one fist. "Hello, Kade. Are you here about Mr. O'Connell?"

"Yes." Lummus's gaze darted between her and Rory. "Peggy, you're as pale as ice. I think you should sit—"

"I'm fine. What about Mr. O'Connell?"

"He went off a cliff in your station wagon, about twenty miles north of here. He's dead. I'm sorry."

"Oh, God." Her hand went to her throat. "I'm sorry, too."

"There's some white paint on the wagon's right rear bumper," Kade continued. "Do you know if it was there when O'Connell borrowed it?"

"I don't know." A crease formed between her dark brows. "I didn't notice the paint, but that doesn't mean it wasn't there."

Her eyes were cool, very cool when they flicked

back to Rory. "So, that's the scene you were insisting on going to when I walked in. Don't let me keep you."

An ache punched into his stomach and up toward his heart. He couldn't leave her like this, not without explaining. Dammit, he needed to explain. He looked at Lummus. "Give us a minute. I want to talk to Peggy alone."

The cop shifted his gaze across the kitchen. "Is that okay with you, Peggy?"

"Mr. Sinclair and I don't have anything to talk about."

Rory took a step toward her. "You need to understand something. I'm not leaving until you and I talk. Alone."

"Wrong," Lummus countered evenly. "You'll leave when Peggy says. Otherwise, I'll advise her to sign a trespassing complaint against you."

Rory flashed him a feral smile. "Good try, pal, but that won't work. I'm a paying guest. Legally, I've done nothing that gives my landlady the right to force me to leave."

"You might be right." Lummus rested a hand on the butt of his holstered automatic. "But if Peggy does sign a complaint, you and I will have to go to the courthouse and let a judge settle things."

Without comment, Rory walked to the counter, lifted the top of the shoe box. Inside were numerous vials containing a clear liquid. Each vial bore a dated label marked "Hopechest" and the initials "CO."

Rory turned, met Lummus's gaze. The Prosperino cop wasn't the only one who could play hardball. "Mrs. Honeywell has discovered evidence significant to an FBI investigation.'' That was a stretch, Rory conceded. After all, he had come to Prosperino on personal time, as a favor to Blake. ''My investigation is classified. That means information is on a need-to-know basis. If I think you need to know what this witness has to say, Sergeant Lummus, I'll let you know *after* I take her statement. I intend to do that right now. I doubt I have to tell you what problems my agency can cause for yours if you knowingly impede a federal investigation.''

A muscle worked in Lummus's jaw as he turned to Peggy. ''If you have a problem being alone with this guy, I'll stay here until he goes.''

She closed her eyes, opened them. ''I'm sorry to involve you in this, Kade. To cause you problems.'' She flicked Rory an icy look. ''To have you threatened in my home. You don't need to stay, Kade. I can handle this.''

''If you decide you need some help, I'll be right outside.'' Lummus walked to the door, pulled it open, then turned. ''I'll wait in my car, Sinclair. You can follow me to the scene. I wouldn't want you to get the idea I'm impeding your investigation.''

''Fine.'' Rory knew he had some fences to mend with the cop.

Peggy walked to the center island, laid the sprig on a cutting board, then looked at him. Despite the fists her hands were clenched in, they were shaking.

Knowing it was probably unwise to try to get closer, he moved to the opposite side of the island. ''I'm sorry—''

''I'm sure you are, Agent Sinclair,'' she interrupted,

very cool, very calm. "It's obvious you never intended for me to find out that you're a cop."

"I was planning on telling you this morning."

"What was wrong with telling me last night?"

He shoved a hand through his hair. "Look, I know I've made a mistake. I should have told you. I just wanted... I just didn't."

Her eyes sparked, shot green fire. "You had no right not to tell me. *No right!*"

"I know that. I know."

Cursing himself for a fool, he turned, looked out the window at the gray drizzle. "Blake called me at the lab in D.C.," he said quietly. "He told me about the water contamination, and said he was fed up with O'Connell's lack of results. And suspicious of him, too. Blake had spotted O'Connell having a clandestine meeting at a hay shed on Hopechest, so Blake figured the guy was up to no good. He asked me to come to Prosperino, represent myself as a private chemist so I could test the water and watch O'Connell. Blake figured the best place I could do that was to check in where O'Connell was staying."

"I don't care how you wound up here." Her voice didn't waver, but her hands were now clenched so hard on the edge of the island that her knuckles showed white. "All I care about is that you leave."

"I'm not going anywhere until we settle this."

"It's settled."

"Like hell." He walked around the island toward her. He couldn't not go to her. "Nothing's settled until you let me explain—"

"*You knew*. You knew how I felt about cops, but that didn't matter."

"It did matter. I was crazy to get my hands on you. The minute you told me how your husband died, about how you'd sworn off cops, I backed away. Dammit, I spent three days avoiding you while going slowly out of my mind."

"I *trusted* you."

"I told you everything I could," he shot back, his hands fisting against his thighs. "I even considered telling you I was a cop, but I couldn't take that chance." Digging deep, he found his control again, softened his voice. Every word he spoke hurt his throat. "I had to assume that if I told you, your behavior toward me would change. I didn't know—*don't know*—what O'Connell was up to. If you suddenly started acting different toward me for no apparent reason, it might have made him suspicious. He could have started thinking you knew something about me that he needed to know. He could have hurt you trying to find out."

"Oh, so, by lying you were *protecting* me." With a sudden angry gesture she jerked off the band tying back her hair. Dark waves tumbled over her shoulders. "How noble of you."

"Dammit, I didn't have a choice!" Her frigid anger helped justify his own. "Has it for once crossed your mind that O'Connell might be the man who attacked you in the greenhouse?"

Surprise dulled the anger in her eyes. "Why? Why would he do that?"

"Maybe he was already inside the greenhouse that day, hiding the shoe box of water samples when you came in. No way could he come up with a believable explanation for being there, so he hid under one of the potting benches. If that's the case, he probably panicked when he heard my car pull in—he might have thought I would come to the greenhouse, too. The fog was as thick as soup that day. He would have known if he made it to the door he could get away without my seeing him, even if I was in the parking lot. His one chance to do that was to put you out of commission for a few minutes so he could get out of there.''

"Maybe it was him." The quiet resignation in her voice reached Rory. "That's not the issue here. You didn't respect me enough to tell me the truth about yourself.''

"Respect has nothing to do with it. I didn't tell you because I couldn't risk O'Connell coming after you. If it was him who attacked you in the greenhouse, that gives you an idea of what he was capable of. And that's not all," Rory continued, jerking his head in the direction of the shoe box. "You think O'Connell hid those water samples because he didn't know what was in them? It's my guess he knew early on what contaminated Hopechest's water, but he had a reason to keep that to himself. If that's the case, he could have clued in Jason Colton, given the doc facts about what those pregnant teens from Hopechest consumed. Instead, those girls are still terrified over what might happen to their babies. If I'm right, O'Connell purposely let everyone in this town suffer because he had some sort of personal agenda. You think he'd have had any qualms where you're concerned?''

"Like you?" she countered. "You knew the truth

about how I felt, but you had your own personal agenda where I'm concerned."

"Stop twisting this around," he said through his teeth. "I did what I thought was right."

"Deceiving me was right for *you*." Her bottom lip trembled. "Jay worked undercover. Do you know what he told me the unwritten cop rule is about undercover work?"

With an oath, Rory grabbed her arms. "I don't—"

"He said you lie. And you use. And you take advantage of anything that's offered. Well, I offered you plenty, but I won't be doing that anymore."

"What happened between us isn't like that." He gave her a light shake. For the first time in years, he felt alone on the inside. Hollow. "I care about you. I feel more for you than I have for anyone else. *Anyone.* Last night was about a lot more than just sex, and you know it."

She jerked out of his hold, took a step back. Then another. "Do you honestly believe there would have been a last night if I had known you were a cop? Do you?"

"No." She was slipping away from him. He was standing only a few feet from her, watching the distance grow by leaps and bounds. "No."

"I didn't just give you my body, Rory. I gave you everything. *Everything,*" she repeated with stinging emphasis. "This morning, it dawned on me..."

"What?" he prompted quietly when her voice hitched. "What dawned on you?"

"That I'm a fool." Her eyes remained dry, but hurt welled in them. "Now that you've lied and used and taken advantage of everything that was offered you, I want you to go. Maybe Blake can put you up at Hope-chest—I really don't care. All I care about is that you get out of my life and my home.''

"Just like that?''

"Yes.''

"Ireland—''

"Now!''

Upstairs, Rory threw his clothes into his leather duffel that sat open on the bed, still rumpled from the hours he had spent with Peggy. Packing was a skill he knew well; he could do it on automatic pilot.

He'd been rejected before, he reminded himself as he grabbed his socks out of the bureau and lobbed them into the bag. His father had sent him away, time and again. After a while, it had no longer hurt. After a while, he had stopped begging to stay where he wasn't wanted. He wouldn't beg now. He'd be damned if he begged.

Even if the events of the morning hadn't taken place, he would have walked away soon. Left for the lab in D.C., or wherever the hell the twists and turns of his job sent him next. No ties, no regrets.

No looking back.

The zipper rasped harshly as he closed the duffel while anger and guilt welled inside him. Placing his unsteady hands on the bed's brass footboard, he tried to stop the pain that stabbed in his gut. He had the sick feeling he had just been shut out of the best thing that had ever happened in his life.

"No.'' His jaw hardened with the word. He didn't

want to stay. Wasn't the kind of man who stayed. He would leave the inn and its landlady, just as he had left dozens of other spots, hundreds of other people.

Hoisting his bag and evidence kit, he turned and stalked out of the room without a look back.

Forty-five minutes later, Rory followed Lummus's black-and-white patrol car around a steep curve, and saw flashing red and blue lights. Cars and vans loomed up ahead, solemnly gathered at the scene of Charlie O'Connell's death.

Rory counted over a dozen vehicles parked along the side of the narrow road that Lummus had accurately described as a nightmare of twists and turns. Towering redwoods crowded one side; the other was lined by a steep face of rough rock that plunged toward the ocean.

The scene looked no different from the hundreds of others Rory had worked. Cops, both uniformed and plain-clothed went about their duties. Just past the spot where Lummus parked, a jump-suited tech used a measuring wheel with a telescoping handle to take the dimensions of a set of skid marks that veered toward the cliff. Another tech crouched over a second set of marks, snapping photographs. Rory knew that, despite the skid marks left by the station wagon, it might be impossible to determine which direction the vehicle had been headed seconds before it plunged toward the sea.

He eased his car in behind Lummus's, then climbed out. He took a minute to pull on his leather jacket against the cool bite of wind that carried the salty tang of the sea. During the drive, the rain had stopped, leaving the sky a bitter blue. Matched his mood, he decided as he retrieved his evidence kit out of the trunk, then strode toward a grim-faced Lummus. Bitter or not, Rory knew he needed to clear the air between himself and the cop so they could do their jobs.

"Look, I apologize for forcing the issue of agency cooperation with you at the inn." As he spoke, Rory sat the kit on the blacktop, pulled out his badge case, flipped it open and anchored it into his jacket pocket. "Nothing personal."

Lummus's brown eyes were flat and cool. "It's pretty obvious what's going on between you and Peggy."

"That's our business."

"I agree. You just need to know that after I'm done here, I'm heading back to Honeywell House. I plan to tell Peggy to give me a call if you show up and she doesn't want you there. That happens, I won't give a damn about agency cooperation. Whatever goes on between you and me will be personal."

"I'm not going back to Honeywell House." Rory forced away the urge to slam his fist into the nearest redwood. He had to compartmentalize his roiling emotions, focus on the job. "After I'm done here, I'm flying those water samples O'Connell had stashed in the greenhouse to the FBI's lab in San Francisco. I want to know what the hell he was up to."

"That's something we agree on." Lummus gestured toward the narrow footpath that led down to the base of the cliff. "After you, Agent Sinclair."

Rory identified himself and gave the name of his agency to the uniformed officer compiling the crime scene log. That done, he and Lummus started down the zigzagging path.

As they edged their way along the sloping cliff, Rory became aware of the heartbeat of the sea. It hit him then how much he would miss driving daily along the coast road to the airport, listening to the thunderous crash of water slapping against rock. His jaw tightened. He would miss a hell of a lot more than just the ocean.

"There it is," Lummus said as he cleared the path's final zigzag.

The black station wagon lay on its side on the small spit of sand, looking like a beached whale. Its front was caved in, the hood crumpled. Rory theorized the wagon had smashed into the beach front-end first, then rolled. He glanced up. He could see only the cliff's jagged face, then the brooding sky. Lummus had been right—if the survey crew hadn't come along, it might have been a while before the wreck was discovered.

Rory noted the lab tech snapping photos of the wagon. He turned, looked at Lummus who had just stepped off the path onto the wet sand. "Are your lab people going to wait to go over the wagon until you get it to your impound lot?"

"That's the plan. One of the techs sealed it after they got O'Connell's body out. The lab guys can do a better job of dusting for prints and vacuuming in their evidence bay."

Rory nodded as they walked. "I'll call you from San Francisco to get an update on what they find. Right now I'm interested in the white paint on the rear bumper." His thoughts went to the white car that Blake had spied parked beside O'Connell's at the hay shed.

"A couple of times, I pulled into the inn's lot and parked behind the station wagon," he continued. "I don't remember seeing white paint on its bumper. I could be wrong—it might have been there. But I don't think so."

Lummus slid him a sideways look. "My guess is, if you didn't notice it, it wasn't there."

Rory settled his evidence kit on one of the craggy rocks that humped out of the sand like an arthritic knuckle. He retrieved his Polaroid and walked to the rear of the station wagon. The wisps of white paint were minimal. Still, he knew they were enough for the lab's sophisticated instruments to establish the exact color, year and make of the vehicle that had left them.

After snapping several photos, he turned to Lummus. "There's not enough paint for me to take samples here. What lab does your department submit its forensic evidence to?"

"The state's crime lab in Sacramento. We usually have to wait a hell of a long time for results."

"Not this time. After your lab techs get the wagon into impound, have them remove the entire bumper and submit it to me."

Lummus gave him a long look. "Submit it where? The FBI lab in San Francisco or in D.C.?"

Rory needed to stay on the west coast. It had nothing to do with the fact that Prosperino had come to mean something to him. Had nothing to do with his feelings for Peggy. He needed to believe that. He had a job to do, had promised Blake answers. That was all.

"San Francisco," he answered. "I'll be there until

I get an ID on the contaminant in Hopechest's water."
He glanced back at the wagon. "Make sure your lab
people pull one of the headlights."

Lummus raised a brow. "Why?"

"In older cars like this where the headlights don't
come on automatically and stay on all the time, checking the condition of a headlight can help establish time
of an accident."

"That's a new one on me."

"If the filament is stretched and broken, that means
the headlights were on. If it's in a tight coil, the lights
were off. It's a good bet no one would try to drive this
road at night without light. You said the M.E.'s aide
estimates O'Connell has been dead at least a day."

"That's right."

"If the wagon's lights were on at the time of impact,
that probably means O'Connell died a couple of hours
after he left the inn."

Turning, Rory walked toward the front of the station
wagon, peered through the shattered windshield. A
foam cup, map and a small, thin box with "Art Kit"
scrawled across its side had been tossed against the
dash. Samantha's art kit. He thought of the possibility
of Peggy and Samantha having been in the wagon
when it plunged off the cliff. Just the thought shattered
his heart.

Fists clenched, he rose, walked back to Lummus.
"Peggy shouldn't be alone, not until we know for sure
who attacked her. Not until I can prove that her station
wagon isn't here because someone thought *she* was behind the wheel."

"You don't need to worry about Peggy," Lummus said. "I'll take care of her."

"Yeah." Rory's stomach twisted at the thought. "I figured you'd say that."

Twelve

Two days later Rory carried a cup of steaming, bottom-of-the-pot coffee and two computer printouts to his borrowed desk in the FBI's San Francisco headquarters. The desk was squeezed into an office that was a little more than an alcove between the trace and drug analysis labs. The alcove was windowless, dimly lit and reeked of the cigarette smoke left by a former occupant. The desk was government-issue decrepit, with flaking gray paint and handles missing from two of its drawers.

Rory didn't care about the size, brightness or scent of the office, the condition of the desk, or that he had forgotten to eat the plastic-wrapped sandwich and bag of chips he'd bought five hours ago from a vending machine. His total concentration was centered on the printouts he had just retrieved from the lab's gas chromatograph, a supermachine that overheats a substance to vapor and then computer-analyzes the gasses to determine chemical composition.

Over the past two days he had introduced separate samples into the chromatograph from each of the vials found in the shoe box Charlie O'Connell had hidden in the greenhouse. Each sample had flowed through various columns and chambers, undergoing a finite series of separation processes, molecular weighing, filtering and amplification. The final detection stage sent information to the chromatograph's computer, which acted as a clearing house that recorded all data produced, and converted electrical impulses into both visual displays and hard copies.

The computer also contained a library of several thousand compounds, which enabled searches that assisted in the identification of unknown compounds.

One of the printouts Rory had settled on the desk in front of him was the final hard copy analysis on all of O'Connell's samples. The second printout showed the results of the computer's comparison of that final analysis to its library of known-compounds.

The second printout drew Rory's immediate attention. He read slowly through the pages showing numerous graphs of compounds that had characteristics similar to the contaminate in Hopechest Ranch's water. When he flipped to the last page, his heart picked up speed. The analysis had come up with an exact match.

After a moment he leaned back in his chair and rubbed his gritty eyes. He now knew the identity of the substance that had contaminated the water on Hopechest Ranch. Knew, too, that the EPA inspector had to have known what it was within days of his arrival in Prosperino.

"Bastard," Rory said through his gritted teeth. He checked his watch, saw it was just after noon. He snatched up the phone, hoping to catch Blake before he left his office for lunch.

After six rings someone picked up on the other end. Rory winced when he heard a hard clatter, then a muffled curse.

"Yeah, what?" Blake's voice came across the line, thick and slurred with sleep. "Hello?"

"What the hell you doing, Fallon?" Rory asked as he reached for his coffee. "Sleeping on the job?"

"Sinclair?"

"Right the first time." Rory took a sip of coffee, then grimaced. If he fed the thick brew through the chromatograph he would probably get a hit in the nuclear range.

"This is important, right? Otherwise you wouldn't be rousting me out of bed at midnight."

"Midnight?" Rory narrowed his eyes. "Hell, I thought it was noon."

"How long since you've gotten out of that lab?"

"I haven't left since I got here two days ago. When I need sleep, I bunk on a couch in a vacant office." Rory glanced around at the small, dim alcove. "It doesn't have a window, either."

"Trust me, it's dark out. My office phone is programmed to ring here after hours."

"I'll take your word for things." As he spoke, Rory raked a palm over his jaw. He had grabbed a couple of quick showers while he'd worked at the lab, but hadn't wanted to waste the time it took to shave. Now the stubble on his face felt like sandpaper.

"I hired you to figure out what's in the water," Blake said, his voice clearing of sleep. "Killing yourself while you're doing that isn't part of the deal."

"The deal's about to close. I've got you an answer."

Blake remained still for a moment, then said, "You found out what the contaminant is?"

"Yes, by using the samples from the box O'Connell stashed. I got an ID about two minutes ago. I haven't had time yet to research the stuff—that'll take me a couple of hours—so I can't answer a lot of questions about it yet."

"What is it, Rory? What the hell is it in Hopechest's water?"

"It's an organic compound. The chemical fingerprint shows it's made up of dimethyl-butyl ether, DMBE for short."

"English, Sinclair."

"Sorry." Rory switched his thoughts out of scientific mode. "DMBE's some sort of gasoline additive. This stuff is new, distinctive. Most of the time when we get a hit on something like this, the computer will give us the name of the company that manufactures it. That didn't happen with DMBE."

"Why not?"

"I don't know. Could be DMBE is still in the testing phases. Maybe more than one company is involved with the stuff. I do know that the petroleum industry is as secretive about their patents as people are about their affairs. If you aren't forced to let out information, you don't."

"Joe Colton owns an oil company," Blake said. "He can probably contact some of his connections and get the ball rolling on finding out what company is behind DMBE."

"If he can, that'll save a hell of a lot of time." Rory paused. "As soon as I wind up things here, I'll fly to Prosperino. Why don't you set up a meeting for this afternoon with Colton and the mayor? Hopefully, I'll know more by then. After that, Longstreet can inform his city council and whoever else he needs to."

"I'll get the meeting set."

"It'll save time if you go ahead and tell Colton and Longstreet that I'm with the FBI. Give them a rundown on your suspicions about O'Connell and why I posed as a private chemist."

"Will do." Blake let out a breath. "You said you got the ID from running the samples O'Connell hid in Peggy's greenhouse?"

"That's right. The samples of water I took two weeks later are what's known as 'weathered.' Over time, the DMBE dissipated so those later samples contain only a finite amount compared to what O'Connell took. I would have gotten the same results on my samples, but my guess is it would have taken a couple more days."

"That means O'Connell must have known about the DMBE weeks ago."

"I'd say so." Suddenly weary, Rory rubbed his fingers between his brows. Two nights with a total of five hours' sleep had left him feeling punchy with fatigue. "While I've been here, I've found out a few more things about the esteemed EPA inspector."

"Anything to make you think that, if the station wagon was forced off the cliff, O'Connell was the intended victim, and not Peggy?"

At the mention of her name, Rory felt his chest tighten. Since she had tossed him out of the inn, he had rigidly controlled his thoughts, kept his mind on business. He had not wanted to deal with the pain that he knew would come if he allowed Peggy to creep into his head.

That she did now had Rory tightening his fingers on the phone. "Yeah, I think O'Connell was the target. I'll give you all the details when I get to Prosperino."

"You still think he's the one who attacked Peggy?"

"Yes. He's the only one who could have hidden those samples in the greenhouse. He was probably checking on them when she came in. Putting her out of commission was the only way he could get out without her seeing him."

"Sounds like we'll have a lot to talk about."

"You're right about that." Rory glanced again at his watch. "I've got to get some sleep before I climb into Longstreet's plane. After that, I'll do some research on DMBE. I'll call you before I leave here so you can let me know where and when we're going to meet."

"Okay. Rory, thanks. I know we have a lot more answers to dig up, like *how* DMBE got into the ranch's water, but this is a start. I appreciate you losing sleep over this."

Rory smiled. "Yeah, well, Fallon, wait until you get my bill."

Blake chuckled. "It'll be a pleasure."

Rory replaced the receiver, rose and strode down the

dim hallway and into the small office where a couch lined one wall. Before, he'd been so engrossed in his work that he hadn't noticed the dark offices, the lack of noise and activity around him. Now he was conscious of the building's eerie stillness.

When he closed the door of the office, a lonely quality permeated the darkness around him. Slowly, he made his way past the desk, sidestepping the two visitors' chairs, finally reaching the upholstered couch against the far wall. He slid off his shoes and stretched out on the soft cushions. With the contaminant identified, the tight leash on which he'd kept his mind slipped away.

Free to wander, his thoughts went straight to Peggy.

He pictured again the anger that had sparked in her green eyes, the betrayal that had welled there.

Rory closed his eyes. He hadn't known how much it would hurt to have her look at him with such pain and fury.

Again, he tasted the panic that had raced through him at the finality in her voice when she'd told him to leave Honeywell House and never come back. Those words should mean little to someone like him. A wanderer. A nomad. A man who had never had a real home. Had never wanted one.

Slowly, he sat up, put his feet on the floor and rested his elbows on his knees. He had never wanted a home, yet Peggy had provided him one. In a few short days she had given him back what had been taken away from him after his mother died. He thought of how many hotels he had slept in alone, of all the people he had walked away from. First, he added grimly. He had shunned emotional entanglements, made sure he was always the one who walked away first. Leaving had always worked because no one had held on to him before. Held on to his heart.

Until now.

Sitting there in the cool, still darkness, Rory felt the truth drop on him like a stone. For the first time in his adult life, his future stretched before him, a barren gray plain. He could travel to hell and back, and never find what he needed. He had already found it, about three hundred miles to the north. In a cozy, charming inn nestled on a hillside in Prosperino, California.

On a low groan, he buried his face in his hands. He couldn't avoid it any longer, he thought. He couldn't keep denying that he had fallen in love with Peggy. It had probably happened the moment he'd stood in the inn's foyer, watching her green eyes shoot fire while she threatened to toss the lech O'Connell out the door.

Rory scrubbed his hands over his face. Okay, so he was in love with Peggy Honeywell. Not only her, he amended when his heart clenched, but her elfin-faced daughter with dark gypsy curls. He loved them both. Wanted them. Problem was, he'd gotten himself tossed out of their lives, which was the one place—the only place—he wanted to be.

Well, Peggy could just forget it, because he wasn't going anywhere. And he wouldn't—by God, he wouldn't—let her walk away from him.

Muttering an oath, he switched on the lamp on the table beside the couch, rose and stalked to the desk. He jerked up the phone, stabbed in the inn's number. After a few rings, the answering machine picked up.

"This is Peggy Honeywell at Honeywell House." The smooth, silky drift of her voice had Rory fisting his frustrated hand at his side. "We're taking a break for a couple of weeks, but are accepting reservations for the middle of February and beyond. Please leave your name and number and I'll get back to you."

When the beep sounded, Rory hung up, scowling at the phone. A couple of weeks? He would be stark-raving crazy in a couple of weeks if he had to go that long without seeing her.

He was a man who had some serious crawling to do, and he didn't feel like waiting. His mouth settled in a firm line. He didn't *have* to wait, not since he knew where she'd gone. She had mentioned closing the inn when he left and taking Samantha to Tahoe where friends had offered the use of their lake house.

Tahoe, he thought.

Late that afternoon Rory sat on the green leather sofa in Blake's office on Hopechest Ranch. Blake sat at the opposite end of the couch. Joe Colton and Mayor Michael Longstreet had each settled into one of the wing chairs that faced the couch across the span of the small coffee table. Blake's secretary, Holly Lamb, had brought in the tray of coffee that sat on the table.

The mayor leaned forward, his face grim. "So, Rory, you're saying there's no way the DMBE could have gotten into Hopechest's water supply naturally?"

"Not in the way you're asking. It's man-made, a gasoline additive, so it didn't fall from the sky when it rained or anything like that. As for whether the DMBE is in the water due to an act of sabotage, I can't answer that until we know if there are underground petroleum pipelines near the aquifer that supplies water to Hopechest. If there are, it's possible the DMBE could have leaked from one of those pipelines."

"There are no pipelines."

Rory met Joe Colton's gaze across the table and decided he had never seen anger so cold, so controlled. "You're sure?" he asked quietly.

"Yes." Joe's hands clenched on his thighs. "The minute we knew there was a problem with the water, I had a couple of people from my oil company start researching records. There aren't any underground oil or gas pipelines on Hopechest property. That means someone dumped the DMBE intentionally."

"Now we have to find out who." Rory shifted his gaze to Blake. "As soon as we're done here, I'll notify the Bureau and the EPA. They should have teams here by morning to start investigating."

Blake's mouth tightened. "Hopechest is under attack, and it could be because of me. Because my dad tried to kill you, Joe. I'm turning in my letter of resignation to the Hopechest Foundation before the close of business today."

"Absolutely not." Joe surged out of the chair. The man might be sixty-one, Rory thought, but he was still a formidable figure with that whipcord build and linebacker shoulders. "You and I have talked about this, Blake. What Emmett did isn't your fault. If some misguided moron dumped the DMBE into the ranch's water to get back at you for that, we'll deal with him when we find him. For whatever reason Hopechest Ranch is suffering, it needs you at its helm. You hear me, Blake?''

"I hear you, Joe. I'm just not sure you're right."

Joe's mouth curved. "Well, son, you can have Holly go to all the trouble of typing your letter of resignation and submitting it to the foundation. The problem with that is Meredith and I sit on the foundation's board of directors. My nephew, Jackson, is the foundation's legal advisor. I imagine he'll find some flaw in your letter so he'll have to recommend to the board that we reject your resignation."

Rory slid Blake a sideways glance. "Looks like you're staying."

"Yeah."

Settling his hands on the back of the chair he had vacated, Joe met Rory's gaze. "Let's get back to O'Connell. You said he should have identified the DMBE a few days after he took the first water samples."

"That's right. The samples I found in Peggy Honeywell's greenhouse are dated the day O'Connell arrived in Prosperino. Because the DMBE is so concentrated in those samples, it took me only two days to ID it."

"So, he had a reason to keep that information to himself."

"Yes. While I waited for the results on the samples, I ran a background check on O'Connell. When he arrived in Prosperino, he was in debt up to his eyeballs. Last week he paid off half the money he owed. He's divorced, has no kids, no immediate family. I can't find any record of a sudden inheritance or anything like that to explain where the money came from." Rory raised a shoulder. "It's possible he took a trip to Vegas and won big there. My instincts tell me that's not what happened."

His dark eyes intent, Michael crossed his arms over his chest. "So, at least on the surface, it appears O'Connell somehow figured out who dumped the DMBE in the water. He confronted that person and told them to pay up or else."

"Yes. I found out O'Connell made a call to the state water commission." Rory didn't add he discovered that by running a check on the phone number he found during his search of O'Connell's room at Honeywell House. "A clerk at the commission said O'Connell asked if there was a schematic of one of the water aquifers near Hopechest. The aquifer was mapped twelve years ago, so the schematic is no longer reprinted, though it's available in the archives. O'Connell showed up there the next day and took a look at that schematic."

Joe rubbed his chin. "Which maybe led him to who-ever dumped the DMBE."

"Possibly," Rory agreed. "Because of O'Connell's unexplained windfall, it looks like that person paid part of the money O'Connell demanded. I say that because it doesn't make sense for him to ask for only half of what it would take to cover his debts. My guess is, he demanded a hell of a lot more and agreed to take the blackmail payments in installments. The meeting he mentioned to Peggy when he borrowed her station wagon was probably to collect more money from the blackmailer. Whoever he or she is made sure

O'Connell wasn't going to be around to talk, or to collect more."

"If your theory pans out, that makes the dumper a murderer," Michael said quietly.

"If I'm right about all of this, it does."

The mayor narrowed his eyes. "You've already told us that a group of ten petroleum companies originally banded together to test DMBE. That means workers in ten different companies have acccss to DMBE. It's going to take the feds time to look at the records of all those companies, run backgrounds on all of their employees, then check them all out."

"True," Rory agreed. "And since we can't come up with a solid motive for why that person dumped the DMBE in the first place, no one can automatically be eliminated from the suspect list."

Michael rose, hooked his thumbs in the front pockets of his jeans. "In the meantime, I've got to figure out how to tell the city council and the rest of the town that the dumping was a criminal act. As long as the possibility existed that the contaminant got into the water through an act of nature, people were willing to stand back and wait for results. When they find out we know for sure someone dumped the contaminant—and could hit Prosperino's water supply next—I might have a full-scale panic on my hands."

Joe laid a hand on Michael's shoulder. "We'll get through this."

Michael gave the older man a wry look. "Have the citizens of Prosperino burned a mayor in effigy anytime in your memory, Joe?"

"No comment."

Shrugging, Michael leaned across the table, offered Rory his hand. "I appreciate the advance notice on this."

Rory rose, returned the mayor's handshake. "And I appreciate the use of your Bonanza." Rory dug into the pocket of his slacks, retrieved the plane's key and handed it to Michael. "You saved me a lot of time and a lot of driving."

"Glad to have been of help. I'm going back to city hall. I need to phone and advise each of the council members of your findings. I'm scheduling an emergency council meeting for tonight. Can you be there to answer whatever questions come up?"

Rory felt a slash of guilt, quelled it. "Sorry, I'm leaving right after I make those calls to the Bureau and the EPA." He caught Blake's knowing look before turning back to Michael. "The three of you know as much about this as I do so far. The fact sheets the EPA sent me cover the short- and long-term effects of DMBE consumption. That's probably going to cover most of the questions you'll get tonight."

Michael angled his head. "What about the pregnant girls?"

Blake rose, stepped around the coffee table. "Just before you got here, I sent Suzanne Jorgenson over to the hospital to outline everything to Doc Colton. You should have seen her face light up when she read on the fact sheet that it takes years of continued exposure to DMBE to cause birth defects."

"Sorry I missed seeing her," Michael murmured, disappointment flashing in his eyes. "She's worried herself sick over the pregnant teens."

Joe offered Rory his hand and a smile. "Glad to have made your acquaintance, Agent Sinclair. Hope you'll make it back to Prosperino someday."

"I'm counting on being back soon." If he could convince Peggy to open her heart to him. He *had* to convince her.

When Joe and Michael strode out the door, Rory headed for Blake's neat-as-a-pin desk. After placing calls to the FBI and EPA to advise both agencies of his findings, he turned to Blake. "Did you find out where the house is at Tahoe?"

"Yes." Blake pulled a piece of folded paper out of his shirt pocket. "The house belongs to Colt and Thea Newman—they own the art gallery just to the west of the movie theater. Peggy caters receptions at their gallery sometimes. Every year they offer Peggy and Samantha the use of their lake house, but Peggy hasn't taken them up on it before. Thea said Peggy called two days ago and asked if their offer was still open."

The day he left. Rory fisted his hands, flexed them. "Do you know what she's driving?"

"No. When I talked to Colt, he mentioned Peggy had rented a car, but he didn't say what kind. He also said the house is out of the way and hard to find." As he spoke, Blake handed the paper to Rory. "Don't lose this."

"You can bet I won't." Rory pulled his leather jacket off one of the visitors' chairs, shrugged it on, then slid the paper into his inside pocket.

Blake angled his chin. "Since you're heading to Tahoe, I guess whatever's between you and Peggy is serious."

"As far as she's concerned, there's nothing between us. I'm hoping to change her mind." He would beg, promise, fight, do whatever it took to put her back into his life.

Turning, Rory strode toward the door, then paused. "Wish me luck," he said over his shoulder.

Blake grinned. "You've got it, pal."

Thirteen

Peggy closed the door on the small, cozy bedroom Samantha had claimed on the lake house's second floor. It had taken at least thirty minutes to steer her daughter's questions away from the topic of "Mr. Rory" and on to the storybook adventures of Barbie.

Pressing her palm against the tightness that had settled around her heart, Peggy walked soundlessly down the staircase into the large living room that was topped by a loft and skylights. The only light in the room came from the flickering flames in the fieldstone fireplace that dominated one wall. Opposite the fireplace was a floor-to-ceiling window that looked out on Lake Tahoe. Tonight the moon was full, its silver light shimmering like a fall of diamonds across the dark water.

A coldness more gray than the dawn seeped into her body, into her very bones, and she heard herself make an anguished little sound. Moving to the fireplace where wood crackled and sparked, she lowered onto the hearth and waited for the fire's heat to sneak through the heavy knit of her sweater.

Over the past two days her anger had died away to misery. Gut-wrenching misery. Here, now, she could admit that what Rory had done had been for her own good. He hadn't kept the fact he was a cop to himself in order to get her into bed. He had remained quiet to protect her from whatever threat Charlie O'Connell presented.

Her thoughts scrolled back to the morning the EPA inspector tripped over Bugs and tumbled down the inn's staircase. The man had stood tight-lipped at the bottom of the stairs, as she'd knelt to comfort a sobbing Samantha. In retrospect, Peggy realized that, for an instant, O'Connell's expression had been almost frightening in its coldness.

Even then, Rory had stepped between them, a protector. If O'Connell was the man who attacked her, Peggy knew without doubt he was capable of much more than cold, killing glares. Rory had sensed that, too.

Rising from the hearth, Peggy skirted around the sofa and armchairs scattered near the fireplace. She roamed past the wall of built-in bookcases, stopping when she reached the expansive window. Wrapping her arms around her waist, she stared unseeingly out at the dark lake.

Would she have acted the same way toward Rory— pursued him—if she had known he wore a badge, just as Jay had? Would she have been strong enough to

turn away from that compelling, intense face and those
killer-blue eyes that held a hint of danger? Could she
have truly resisted the desire that had clawed at her
since the first moment she had laid eyes on him?

It didn't matter, she told herself. She hadn't resisted.
Sure hadn't been forced. She'd gone after what she
wanted, taken it. Now she had to deal with the consequences of her actions.

Which was the real reason she'd closed the inn and
brought Samantha to Tahoe. Here, away from the place
where memories of Rory assaulted her at every turn,
she would heal. Get her balance back.

And get over the infatuation she'd mistaken for love.
She didn't love Rory Sinclair, she told herself, stiff-
ening her shoulders. Wouldn't let herself love a man
who had probably already wiped all images of her from
his mind. A man who excelled at leaving.

She, too, was determined to set her sights on the
future, not the past.

A sudden, sharp knock on the front door shot her
heart into her throat. Only a few people knew she and
Samantha were staying at the cabin. Peggy was expecting none of them.

Veering toward the fireplace, she grabbed the brass
poker from its holder. Clenching its thick handle, she
willed her legs to stop shaking as she edged cautiously
toward the door.

When she peered out the window and saw Rory
standing in the pool of the porch light, her already unsteady legs almost gave out. He was wearing his leather
bomber jacket over an ice-blue sweater and dark slacks.

His dark hair was mussed; his face stubbled by several days growth of beard.

He looked exhausted and grim-faced.

Slowly, she pulled the door open. "I wasn't expecting you," she said without expression.

"I know." His gaze flicked to her hand. "Garden shears, fireplace poker. You always choose interesting weapons, Ireland."

"How...did you find me?"

His mouth lifted at the corners. "I don't think I need to remind you that I'm a cop."

"No." Her throat felt rusty; she braced a hand on the door for balance. "I came here to spend time with my daughter. I don't want you here."

"Too bad." In one smooth move he pulled the poker from her grasp, leaned it against the wall, then locked his hands on her shoulders and nudged her back. "Right now I don't give a damn if you want me here or not," he added as he used one foot to swing the door shut behind him. "I need to talk to you."

"We've already said all there is to say to each other." She had to clamp her hands on his upper arms to keep from stumbling while he steered her backward.

"Like hell. I just drove like a maniac across this entire state so I can have my say." He forced her downward onto the couch that faced the fireplace. "You're going to listen."

Emotion tightened her throat; air clogged her lungs. She couldn't have spoken if her life depended on it.

He yanked off his jacket, lobbed it into the nearest chair, then stared down at her, his face grim. "Do you know how many people can't make a home? How many don't have a clue how to nurture their own children?"

Peggy puffed out a surprised breath. She wasn't sure what she had expected him to say, but that wasn't it. "Millions of people make homes and nurture their children."

"The people I knew didn't," he said fiercely. "My father sent me away after my mother died. After a while, I stopped hurting over that. I wouldn't let myself hurt. And I wouldn't let myself want what had been taken away from me." She saw the raw emotion in his eyes as he took a step toward her. "The night I walked into the inn, you gave that back to me. You gave me a home."

"Which you don't want."

He held up a hand. "I need to get through this. Let me get through this. Please."

"All right."

"Not only did I not want a home, I didn't want to feel anything for you." He stood facing her, his eyes smoldering with the same intensity as the flames in the fireplace. "I kept telling myself you were like every other woman whose path I had crossed over the years. The harder I worked to convince myself of that, the more obvious the truth became. Still, I didn't want to think you made a difference. Didn't want to believe I couldn't leave you as easily as I have everyone else. When you kicked me out of the inn, I found out I was wrong. For the first time in my life I left a part of myself behind."

In her heart, she thought, feeling something move inside her. That part of him had stayed behind in her heart. Tears welled as her mind accepted what she'd fought so hard over the past days to deny. She loved him.

"I never meant to hurt you." He shoved a hand through his dark hair. "I kept the fact I'm a cop secret to protect you. Someday I hope you'll be able to trust that. I hope you'll believe that I did what I did because I love you."

She jolted. "You—" She rose slowly. "What did you say?"

Before she could gather her wits, he moved to her, took one of her hands in his own. "I love you and I love Samantha."

She had to take a step back, had to press a hand against the pressure in her chest. "Why did you have to tell me that? Damn you, why?"

His grip tightened, along with his voice. "Okay, I guess the feeling isn't mutual. Tough luck for me. But that's how I feel."

She jerked from his hold, clenched her hands into fists. "So, you drove like a maniac across the state to tell me you *love* me?"

His eyes narrowed. "That, and a couple of other things. I thought they were important. Maybe you've got a different spin on that."

"Do you think it makes it easier for me, knowing how you feel? Knowing the man I've fallen in love with loves me back? That somewhere roaming around the globe is some idiot with rocks in his head who loves me, but doesn't want a life with me?"

"Hold on." He stepped forward. "You love me? Did I hear you right? You mean it?"

"Yes, and a hell of a lot of good that does me."
She crammed her hands on her hips. "You've made
sure I understand who you are, *what* you are. 'I'm a
nomad,'" she tossed out, lowering her voice to imitate
his. "'I don't stay in one place. Leaving is what I do,
what I'm good at. I can throw everything I own into
my plane and take off without looking back. Ever.'"
She dragged in a breath. "It would have been a lot
easier for me to get over you if I thought you didn't
care."

"I don't want you to get over me." Closing the
space between them, he brought a hand to her face,
skimming back her hair with his fingers, molding her
jawline with his palm. "For the last six months I've
felt this...restless discontent, like my life had gotten
off track. I couldn't put my finger on what had happened. I think it's because I was ready to find a place
I belong, one place that means something to me. Someone who means something to me." His eyes eloquent,
he slid his palm around to cup the back of her neck.
"Even if you tell me to leave again, I won't. I'm staying in Prosperino. I have to stay. I *need* to stay. I need
to convince you to let me back into your life."

Her breath hitched with joy; tears streamed down her
cheeks.

"Don't cry." He thumbed away her tears. "For
God's sake, Ireland, don't cry. My job isn't like Jay's
was. I do most of my work in a lab. I visit crime scenes
after the fact." He shook his head. "But, if you want
me to give it up, I will. I'm crazy about you. You're
the only woman I've ever wanted to spend my life

with. I'll do whatever it takes to have you and Samantha back in my life, for the rest of my life."

Her heart overflowed. He loved her and Samantha. Wanted them. He would stay.

She settled her palm against his chest, felt the reassuring beat of his heart. "When you left, I felt the same kind of emptiness I did when Jay died." Tears burned her throat, thickening her voice. "I would have felt that way, no matter what you did for a living. I didn't fall in love with the badge. I fell in love with the man. I don't want you to go. I don't want you to stop being a cop."

He gathered her close, dipped his head and skimmed his mouth across hers. "The lab in San Francisco has an opening. I have my plane. I can commute there every day and come home every night. Let me come home to you, Ireland."

"Yes." She couldn't get enough of him as she tasted, touched as if she had never known a man before. In that moment she could remember no others. Only him.

Smiling up at him, she lifted a hand to his cheek. "Welcome home."

Don't miss any of
the Colton family saga. Pick up
SWEET CHILD OF MINE
by Jean Brashear in June 2002.

One

She ran the fingers of one hand through the long, silky mane and tried to smile. "Jim said it was too bad I couldn't just order up a husband. He thinks he could get the cousin to back off if he could show her that I could give Bobby as much as she could." She glanced up at Michael. "Know any likely candidates, Counselor? Since you're on retainer and all, might as well get my money's worth." She strove for lightness, but in her eyes, pure misery swam.

Michael thought about his conversation with his mother and almost laughed, except it wasn't funny. Just hours ago, he'd been gnashing his teeth, wishing for a way to ease his father's last days but unable to stomach the hypocrisy of searching for a temporary wife.

He shook his head. Surely he couldn't seriously be

considering the obvious option. He had the solution for both of them right in his hands, but mama mia—

But he knew he couldn't rule it out. Fate was a quirky, ill-tempered witch, but every once in a while, she smiled your way. "What would you do with this husband if you found him?" He strove for a casual tone.

"I'd kiss his feet if he'd help me get my son."

"You only want a man long enough to get custody of your child, is that it?" He didn't know why that pricked at his temper. It was perfect. All he wanted was a way to make his dad happy during whatever time remained. He had no heart left to give a woman.

But she didn't look cynical. Just worn and said, "My only concern has to be Bobby right now. But it doesn't matter, anyway. There's no candidate running around."

Michael took a quick glance out the window, wondering if he could really do this.

Then he looked back at the woman across from him, and the slope of defeat in her shoulders tugged at his conscience. He could help her out and make his dad happy at the same time. She didn't want more than he could give. All her love would go to her son. If he were the one dying and having to leave a son behind, he'd want that son to have a mother's love as fierce as Suzanne's.

He turned back to study her closely. "Maybe there is."

Her head jerked up. Her eyes narrowed. "That's not funny, Michael. Please—I don't feel like sparring now."

"I'm not sparring. And I'm not joking. Maybe I've got a solution for you."

Any hesitation he felt was doomed, once he saw the flare of intense joy in her eyes. Quickly, she banked it, holding herself stiffly as if afraid to trust his words. Her tone was guarded as she responded. "And what might that solution be?"

Here goes nothing. He felt a swift inner clench as he opened his mouth to speak.

"You could marry me."

SILHOUETTE *Romance*

Escape to a place where a kiss is still a kiss...
Feel the breathless connection...
Fall in love as though it were
the very first time...
Experience the power of love!

Come to where favorite authors——such as
Diana Palmer, Stella Bagwell,
Marie Ferrarella and many more——
deliver heart-warming romance and genuine
emotion, time after time after time....

Silhouette Romance——
stories straight from the heart!

Silhouette®
Where love comes alive™

Visit Silhouette at www.eHarlequin.com.   SRDIR1

INTIMATE MOMENTS™
Romance, Adventure—Excitement

IF YOU'VE GOT THE TIME...
WE'VE GOT THE INTIMATE MOMENTS

Passion. Suspense. Desire. Drama.
Enter a world that's larger
than life, where men and women
overcome life's greatest odds
for the ultimate prize: love.
Nonstop excitement is closer
than you think...in
Silhouette Intimate Moments!

Where love comes alive™

Visit Silhouette at www.eHarlequin.com

SIMDIR1

passionate powerful provocative love stories that fulfill your every desire

Silhouette Desire delivers strong heroes, spirited heroines and stellar love stories.

Desire features your favorite authors, including

Diana Palmer, Annette Broadrick, Ann Major, Anne MacAllister and Cait London.

Passionate, powerful and provocative romances *guaranteed!*

For superlative authors, sensual stories and sexy heroes, choose Silhouette Desire.

Available at your favorite retail outlet.

Where love comes alive™

passionate powerful provocative love stories that fulfill your every desire

Visit us at www.eHarlequin.com   SDGEN00

♥ *Silhouette*

SPECIAL EDITION™

Emotional, compelling stories that capture the intensity of living, loving and creating a family in today's world.

Special Edition features bestselling authors such as Nora Roberts, Diana Palmer, Sherryl Woods, Lindsay McKenna, Joan Elliott Pickart— and many more!

For a romantic, complex and emotional read, choose Silhouette Special Edition.

Available at your favorite retail outlet.

Where love comes alive™

Visit Silhouette at www.eHarlequin.com   SSEGEN00

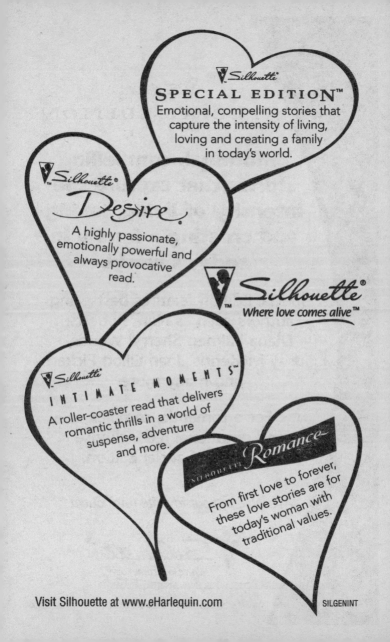

V Silhouette

SPECIAL EDITION™

Emotional, compelling stories that
capture the intensity of living,
loving and creating a family
in today's world.

V Silhouette®

Desire

A highly passionate,
emotionally powerful and
always provocative
read.

V Silhouette®

Where love comes alive™

V Silhouette

INTIMATE MOMENTS™

A roller-coaster read that delivers
romantic thrills in a world of
suspense, adventure
and more.

SILHOUETTE Romance

From first love to forever,
these love stories are for
today's woman with
traditional values.

Visit Silhouette at www.eHarlequin.com

SILGENINT

Where love comes alive™

From first love to forever, these love stories are
for today's woman with traditional values.

A highly passionate, emotionally powerful
and always provocative read.

SPECIAL EDITION™

Emotional, compelling stories that capture the
intensity of living, loving and creating a family in
today's world.

INTIMATE MOMENTS™

A roller-coaster read that delivers romantic thrills
in a world of suspense, adventure and more.

Visit Silhouette at www.eHarlequin.com

SDIR2

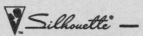

where love comes alive—online...

eHARLEQUIN.com

shop eHarlequin

♥ Find all the new Silhouette releases at everyday great discounts.

♥ Try before you buy! Read an excerpt from the latest Silhouette novels.

♥ Write an online review and share your thoughts with others.

reading room

♥ Read our Internet exclusive daily and weekly online serials, or vote in our interactive novel.

♥ Talk to other readers about your favorite novels in our Reading Groups.

♥ Take our Choose-a-Book quiz to find the series that matches you!

authors' alcove

♥ Find out interesting tidbits and details about your favorite authors' lives, interests and writing habits.

♥ Ever dreamed of being an author? Enter our Writing Round Robin. The Winning Chapter will be published online! Or review our writing guidelines for submitting your novel.

All this and more available at
www.eHarlequin.com
on Women.com Networks

SINTB1R